MW00772140

A View to a Kiln

**A Harry's
Pottery Mystery**
by Holly Jacobs

A View to a Kiln

Copyright © 2022 by Holly Fuhrmann
Ilex Books

Dedication:
For Tom Hubert—
A wonderful professor who gave me
the gift of clay.
Thank you for not batting an eye
when I started a question with,
"Say I wanted to burn up a body in a
kiln..."

Dear Reader,

I started Mercyhurst University in 2017. I took exactly one class. Ceramics.

I loved it!

My professor and the rest of the class put up with my overflowing enthusiasm. The kids were so kind. I know this for a fact because when I got back my "building" project, a Hobbit Hole, and it didn't explode in the kiln, I gave a little squeal of glee then apologized for my enthusiasm. I assured them that I tried to keep it under wraps. Uh, they told me I didn't keep it under wraps very well at all...but they didn't hold that against me.

I exhausted every pottery class Mercyhurst had to offer. (*After my last class, the professor retired. My kids have assured me they think there's a chance I just wore him out.*)

After that, I built my own pottery studio, HollysWoods Studio. Yes, I built it in the woods. These days I split my time between writing, claying, and family. Not in that order.

I've written a lot of romance, women's fiction, and one other cozy mystery series, Maid in LA. I'm happy to say this book combines the romance and the cozy mystery...and pottery.

I hope you enjoy Harry's Pottery, *A View to a Kiln*. I'll give you a hint, there's a kiln and a dead body.

Thanks to all my social media followers who put up with my pottery, books, and cottage glee with as much patience as all the kids who shared all those classes with me.

Holly

A View to a Kiln

**A Harry's
Pottery Mystery**
by Holly Jacobs

Prologue

"The truest definition of ART is our dreams made manifest."
~Harry's Pottery: A Personal Journey

"I'm not happy. I deserve to be happy, so I'm leaving you."

Alex's words were the beginning of my journey.

No, that's not true.

The very beginning of my journey was an art requirement for my undergrad degree at Mercyhurst University. I chose a ceramics class because I thought it would be an easy class.

It was *not* an easy class, but it was a class that changed my life.

That class is what led to *this* moment, even more than Alex's declaration of unhappiness had.

I looked at the two-story brick building on West Front Street.

I'd bought it a year ago. Twelve months to the day.

Two months after Alex announced his quest for happiness.

He'd offered to let me keep our South Shore home, but instead, I bought this building on a short sale.

Erie, Pennsylvania had implemented all sorts of new incentive programs to resurrect derelict properties within the city limits. This property had been vacant for years and the bank let it go for a song.

It had great bones. That's what my real estate agent had said.

Bones were about all the house had going for it when I bought it. And bricks. And a porch. I love brick buildings and I love porches.

Now?

I'd spent months working with an architect to perfect the design. Months of demolition. Months renovating the property. I didn't have to consult anyone about anything. Everything was just as I wanted it...just as I'd envisioned it the day the real estate agent let me inside.

I set up my first-floor ceramic studio and storefront exactly the way I wanted. And while I'd paid less attention to the design of the small apartment upstairs, even that was cozy and functional and rehabbed to my taste.

But today was my real new beginning.

My divorce was official, and the crew was serendipitously hanging my new sign.

Harry's Pottery.

I'd debated over the name, but Harriet's Pottery didn't have the same ring. And Lawe's Pottery sounded far too legal for my taste. I'd gone back to my maiden name after Alex Murphy left me. So, Murphy's Pottery wasn't even an option.

I had one last step before I started this new chapter of my life. The chapter my ex-husband's I-deserve-to-be-happy comment had inspired.

I deserved to be happy as well.

I snapped pictures as the crew hung the sign from the front porch.

Harry's Pottery.

This studio and storefront were my path to happiness.

When the sign crew left, so did I.

I went to my father's office in a regal West Sixth building, parked in my spot and went inside.

I packed up my desk, took the box to my car and then walked into my father's office at precisely 1 p.m.

"Harriet," he said as I opened his door.

He checked his watch to be sure I was on time.

"Father," I said formally. Formal was my father's middle name.

Okay, so his middle name was really Osborn, but it should have been *Formal.*

I could imagine him as a toddler, dressed in a suit and carrying a briefcase to preschool.

"Have a seat," he invited. "You had something you wished to discuss?"

The door opened and Perkins, my father's assistant, said, "Mr. Lawe, John Michael called and—"

My father dismissed poor Perkins without saying a word.

"Harriet?" he said again, prompting me to tell him what this meeting was about.

"Last year when Alex asked for a divorce, he said he deserved to be happy and I didn't make him happy any longer...well, that stung. But his words stayed with me. I've thought a lot about it and realized that no one could have made Alex happy. He got his divorce and last time I saw him, he didn't seem overly..." I paused.

"Happy?" my father supplied dryly.

"Exactly. It's up to each of us to find our own happiness. Finding work that fulfills us is a good place to start." I took a deep breath then blurted out, "You see, I've found mine—"

"I'm glad the law firm makes you happy," my father said.

That was a rare fatherly thing for him to say. For a moment, I questioned my decision, but the moment passed quickly. I knew I was doing what was right for me. My father wouldn't approve, but he'd adjust.

"I tried to remember the last time I was completely happy. I kept coming back to being in school, taking Ceramics with Professor Bert."

My father froze now. His eyes pinned me as if I were a witness he was about to cross-examine or a butterfly being pinned to a board. It was hard to move under the weight of his gaze. Harder still to put coherent thoughts into words.

But I'd practiced for just this moment. "I loved wedging the clay, preparing it to become something else entirely. I loved having an idea of what I wanted to make and then watching it become something solid and real. I loved glazing. There was something magic about painting the dull looking glazes onto a piece and seeing what came out of the kiln. I—"

"Harriet, I'm pleased the little studio you're building at your new place is making you happy," he said slowly. I think he suspected what I was going to say and didn't want to hear it.

Josiah Osborn Lawe, Esquire hadn't wanted to hear it years ago when I was in college and he didn't want to hear it now.

After that first class with Professor Bert, I decided to become an art major. I worked it all out in my head. I'd get an education degree as well. My father would respect the idea of teaching. That's how I'd win him over. I'd teach art as my job, and I'd do art as my passion.

Alas, I didn't win anything.

I graduated college with a degree Political Science and a minor in Spanish. And four ceramic classes under my belt. I went to law school, came home and went to work at Lawe and Associates.

"Father, I quit." I slid my formal resignation letter across the desk to him.

"Harriet—"

"I love you. But I don't love this job. And that's the one gift Alex left me with. I deserve to be happy, Father."

My father sat stone still, as if formulating an argument for a jury.

I took advantage of the moment, got up, walked around the desk and kissed his cheek. "I've already cleared up most of my work and handed off the rest. I'll see you at brunch on Sunday."

I walked to the door and said, more to myself than to my father, "I deserve to be happy."

Chapter One

"Making something in clay is tangible. You can see what you're getting. But glaze is always a surprise. You never know what to expect."
~Harry's Pottery: A Personal Journey

One year.

One year after my marriage fell apart, I'd hung my Harry's Pottery sign.

On that day, I'd walked into my father's office and resigned.

For one year, I'd been living my dream.

All right, so some days the dream was rather drudge-like.

I was almost finished with a wholesale order, which was *very* drudge-like. It wasn't the most creative work, but it kept the electricity on.

I'd spent the last two days throwing bowls off the hump. Basically, I took a huge lump of clay on my wheel and made one bowl, cut it off, made another, cut it off, made another....

It had taken me months to master the process, but it was worth learning because it saved a lot of time on big orders like this.

Today was going to be another *Hump Day*, even though it was a Thursday not a Wednesday.

I smiled at my own mental quip as I poured my morning cup of coffee and headed towards the back door that led to the narrow staircase between my apartment and my studio. My cellphone rang, stopping me in my tracks.

"Good morning, Miss Betty," I managed to croak with my un-coffee lubricated throat.

"Harry?" my neighbor said, sounding surprised I knew it was her. She always sounded surprised that I knew it was her before she said a word.

Betty Abler lived next door. She'd lived in the house for fifty years, long before the Front Street neighborhood began gentrifying. She'd lived there before they'd put in the bayfront promenade and started to revitalize the entire bayfront area. Miss Betty had moved here back when the row of houses facing the bay constituted a simple family neighborhood.

Miss Betty used a landline with no Caller I.D. and never understood how I knew it was her on the line.

"Yes, Miss Betty, it's me," I assured her.

"I just wanted to be sure we were still going to the grocery store tonight?"

I'd convinced Miss Betty that she should give up her car after she crashed into her garage door...for a second time. I'd been driving her on errands ever since. Thursdays were our grocery nights most weeks.

Front Street was a lovely neighborhood in the truest sense. We'd had a storm of the century last winter. More than eighty inches of snow in December. The neighbors had all pitched in and helped each other dig out over and over again. I hadn't been the only one to check on Miss Betty, our oldest neighbor. We all considered her the matriarch of Front Street.

"I'm definitely still shopping," I assured her. "I'm planning sushi for dinner. I'll come over as soon as I close the shop."

"Thanks, honey," she said.

"See you later." I took a long sip of coffee and headed down the back staircase. The apartment's front stairs led to the front door, a door I hardly ever used. It was on the west side of the porch.

My studio was in the back of the first floor and the retail space was in the front. Because ceramics was a dusty art, a big plate-glass window separated the two areas. The glass allowed me to see customers come in while I worked which meant I didn't have to sit idly by between customers. The glass also kept the dust in the studio.

When I'd first opened, there were very long periods between customers. The last few months there'd been a lot more foot traffic. I was hoping as we got closer to the holiday shopping season, things would really take off.

I'd spent a week making small Christmas trees and another week making some very folk-artsy Santas. I'd already sold enough of both to make sure I'd make even more of both next year.

The retail space didn't make enough money to fully support me, but when added to my wholesale work, like these bowls, and my round of craft sales, I made a living. When things got tight, I still did occasional contract work for my father's firm.

It might be a piecemeal living, but it was a comfortable living.

And I was happy.

I thought about my ex and smiled.

Mission accomplished.

I was still grinning as I took another sip of coffee and opened the door at the bottom of the staircase. I flipped on the lights as I entered the studio.

I gulped the sip of coffee down and tried to resist gagging as I was hit by a wave of stench. A truly disgusting odor the likes of which I'd never smelled before. It was like something awful and rank being fried. Now, firing up ceramics in a kiln wasn't the best smell ever, but I wasn't running a kiln.

I had a huge fan in the kiln room which helped and I normally only ran it on weekends just to avoid the odor, but it was a bed of roses compared to what I was smelling now.

No, this stench was definitely not a kiln smell.

I set my coffee down on a shelf and looked around. I didn't see anything out of order, and certainly not something that would produce this stench.

I opened the kiln room and was surprised to see the lid on my electric kiln closed. I held my breath and looked closer. It was running.

I hadn't started it.

Maybe it was malfunctioning? Maybe the smell was the kiln burning itself up?

And since I hadn't started it, the exhaust fan wasn't running.

My kiln room was separate from my workroom and when a kiln was firing, I always turned on the fan, venting the room to the outside.

I flipped on the fan, looked at the kiln. It was still only five hundred degrees.

I put on my safety glasses and peered through peephole. There was a series of holes down the entire side of the kiln. I could unplug whichever one I wanted.

I leaned forward and...I simultaneously screamed and jumped back, bumping into my shelf, making the greenware on it rattle.

There wasn't anything ceramic in the kiln.

No, I'd been looking at a skeleton.

More precisely, a skull that I assumed from its height was attached to a skeleton.

For a few moments, I just stood there, dazed.

I was trying to think through mud.

Or clay if you will.

And I regained enough of my wits to turn off the kiln, leave the room, shutting the door behind me.

Safe in my studio, I picked up the phone and dialed 911.

"Hello. What is the nature of your emergency?" said a dispassionate female voice on the other end of the line.

"I..."

I was at a loss on how to describe the nature of my problem.

"I came down to my studio this morning and my electric kiln was running, and the workspace stunk, and I went in and looked and there appears to be a body in my kiln."

That was a lot of ands I thought inanely.

Inane was the best I could do, given the skeleton in my kiln.

"Pardon?" the operator asked.

"Someone put a body in my kiln. All that's left is a skeleton. I mean, I saw a skull and glimpsed more bones, so I think it's a whole skeleton. The kiln read five hundred degrees so I'm not sure what the state of the bones are in at that temperature. I..." I was pretty sure I was going to be sick. "Please send someone."

I managed to spit out my address before I went to the bathroom and indeed threw up.

After which, I called my father.

It had been a year since I resigned from the firm and, finally over the last few months, things had been a bit better. He was still cool towards me, but cool was better than frosty. I knew that even if he was Antarctica frosty, he'd come running if I called.

"Yes, Harriet?" he asked without preamble.

"Dad," I said and tried to search for the right words. "There was a body in my kiln this morning," I blurted out.

My father had always been completely unflappable. We lost my mother three days after I turned fifteen. I started my period three months after that. I was seriously the last girl in my class to get her *monthly visitor*. When I asked my father to add feminine hygiene products to the grocery list, he hadn't so much as blinked. He'd simply asked if I had questions. I assured him I was fine.

I wasn't fine now.

"Did you call the police?" he asked.

"Yes. Can you come?" I needed him more now than I'd ever needed him.

"I'm in court, but I'll send someone," he said.

I was crushed.

My father wasn't going to come.

Rationally, I knew that he couldn't just leave court. But irrationally I wanted him to throw everything else aside and come.

"Never mind." I hung up. "I'll be fine."

I didn't want someone else, I wanted my father. I wanted him to put his arms around me and tell me everything was going to be all right.

Okay, imagining my father hugging me and comforting me like that was a stretch. He had patted my shoulders when my mother died. It had been awkward, but I knew that was the best he could do. He loved me, but he was not a demonstrative man.

Awkward or not, his presence would have given me some comfort. And he would have maybe said it would all be all right.

I wouldn't believe him, but I'd feel better having heard those words.

I didn't have time to wallow in my father's lack of support because there was a knock on my door and the police were standing on the porch.

Two police officers. One was medium height and had weak-tea colored hair and complexion. The other was taller and darker. Both looked stern. "You called 911?" the shorter one asked.

"Yes. I'm so glad you're here," I said. "Being just a few blocks from the police station is a bonus that I'd never thought about until now. I guess it takes finding a body in your kiln to make you realize how important proximity to the police can be. And I—"

First, I couldn't find the words, now I couldn't stop words—any words—from flowing from my mouth like a babbling brook. Thankfully, the taller cop stopped me. "Ma'am, could you tell us what happened and show us the body?"

"I came down this morning to go to work—I have an apartment upstairs—and smelled something awful. Sniff. You can still smell it. I went into the kiln room and found it running. I hadn't started it and thought it must be malfunctioning. I figured that's what I was smelling. I turned on the exhaust fan then I looked inside and there it was..." I shuddered and thought I might throw up again.

"Can you show us?" the shorter one prompted.

I nodded as I convulsively swallowed, trying to keep myself from barfing on the floor.

I led them into the kiln room. The fan was doing its job. Oh, the entire place still smelled, but not nearly as bad as it had initially.

"Can you open it?" he asked.

"I don't know. I don't normally open my kiln while it's hot because it can shock the ceramic pieces. My rule of thumb is not to open it until it's under two hundred degrees at the hottest. I have no idea if opening it while it's still at five hundred plus with bones in it will damage them. I mean, damage them more than firing them has already damaged them. I wasn't a trial lawyer when I practiced law, but I'd have to think you want to preserve whatever you can of the corpse, so I think you'd want to let it cool slowly, then have a coroner or doctor or fire investigator..." I shrugged. "Someone medically vested in examining bones examine them. You'd want them here when you open it to see them before you open it."

That sounded convoluted, but it was the best I could do under the circumstances.

"You're a lawyer?" the cop asked.

"I was. Well, technically, I guess I still am. But I'm really just a potter and I..."

Someone banged on my door, interrupting a new bout of word vomit.

"Should I get that?" I asked.

"Yeah," the tall cop said with a grunt. "I think I'd better make some calls."

"Okay." I walked to the door and saw a man in a suit there. He looked vaguely familiar, but I couldn't place him.

I opened the door. "Yes?"

"Harriet, your father sent me."

Oh, that's how I knew him. He was one of the new guys dad hired after I left the firm. I searched for his name. "Micah?"

"Yes. Did you talk to the cops?" he asked as he came in without a by-your-leave.

"I took them back to the kiln room and showed them what was left of the body."

"Did they ask for your alibi?" he asked.

"My alibi?" I was back to thinking through clay.

"Harriet, you have a body in your kiln. They're going to want an alibi from you."

"Wait a minute. You mean, you think they're going to think that I did that?" I'd been out of the law game for a year, other than the contracts I occasionally worked on for my father when pottery income was less than forthcoming. But other than that, I didn't think like an attorney anymore.

Once Micah said the words, I realized I should have thought of that.

I had a body in my kiln. Of course, the police would need to ask about my alibi. They'd want to know about my day. They'd check into my background.

"Tell me," Micah said softly. He put his hand under my elbow and led me to the bench that sat by the door. "Tell me about yesterday."

"I am an attorney," I said, needing to remind myself more than him.

"You know what they say...an attorney who represents himself has a fool for a client."

"*Herself,*" I corrected. "Or maybe *themselves* to be gender neutral."

"Let me help," Micah said. "Do you have a dollar?"

I reached in my change cup, a small brown cup with a raised sunflower on it and gave him four quarters. "What do you need?"

"My retainer." He dropped the change in his pocket. "Now tell me about yesterday."

"There's nothing to tell. I worked on an order all day. The pieces are drying on the shelf now. I had a handful of customers, which was good for a Wednesday. Saturdays are my biggest days in the storefront. When I closed the doors, I went upstairs, made dinner and watched *The Marvelous Mrs. Maisel* on Amazon Prime. I don't know how I missed it when it first came out, but it's delightful."

Micah stared at me waiting for more.

"I don't have any other alibi," I told him. "I was home alone all night. And my home is directly over the studio. I'm supposed to take a neighbor to the grocery store after work today, but even if that had been yesterday, it would have been a late afternoon alibi at best. I was here alone all night."

"Did you have any phone calls or texts? Were you active online?"

I shook my head. "Nothing. I didn't have any phone calls until this morning when Miss Betty called about a ride."

He sighed as if my alibi, or lack thereof, was disappointing and somehow my fault.

That annoyed me.

"If I'd have known I'd find a dead body in my kiln this morning, I'd have gone to a bar and picked up someone to spend the night with me so I'd have an alibi."

He apparently didn't find my outburst amusing.

I didn't know what else to say, so I said nothing.

I'd had a professor in law school who was a big proponent of saying nothing and pregnant pauses. *Sometimes silence speaks volumes* he used to say.

I nodded at Micah, indicating he should follow me and we walked back toward the kiln room.

"We called the coroner and he agreed we should wait to open the kiln until he gets here," Officer Shorty said.

"Good."

Suddenly I looked at both the officers differently. Officer Shorty and Officer Tall weren't here to save me, they were here to investigate the dead body and I was going to be part of that investigation—a focus of it, at least at first.

"Can you walk us through what happened?" Officer Tall said.

"There's not much to say. I came downstairs this morning with a cup of coffee and something smelled. I came in here and the fan was off and the kiln was on. I didn't start the kiln and when I looked in I found a body staring out at me."

"And then?" Officer Shorty prompted.

"I called 911, threw up, and then I called my father."

"And her father sent me," Micah added.

"And you are?" Officer Tall asked, slightly antagonistic.

"Her attorney," Micah said, matching the officer's antagonism.

"I thought you were a lawyer?" Officer Tall said to me. It was half a question and half an accusation.

"I am. I was." And then I remembered my only bit of alibi. "Oh, and I talked to Miss Betty on my way down here. She's my neighbor. She wanted to check we were going to the store after work. She doesn't drive anymore."

"Who was in the place yesterday?" Officer Shorty said.

"It was busier than most Wednesdays. But no one other than me was in the studio. Customers are in the storefront, except when I'm giving a class. Students use this area." I pointed to the two long tables students used.

"We'd like you to give us a consent to search the studio and your apartment," he said.

I had nothing to hide, and even if I did, the police would be able to get a search warrant with very little effort since I had a body in my kiln.

"Sure," I said.

I signed the consent paper they handed me.

"I can clear a seat for you in the shop," Officer Shorty said.

What he meant is he'd search that area first then have us sit there so I wouldn't have time to mess with any evidence.

I shook my head. "That's not necessary. We'll just go outside and wait. I imagine you'll want me to stay someplace else for a few days while you finish going over everything. When you've made your first pass, could I get in and pack a suitcase and get my purse?"

"Sure," Officer Shorty said.

"Oh, and please, there are shelves in the kiln room full of greenware. That's unfired clay and very delicate. I understand you'll be looking at them, but they're part of a big order. I'm going to be behind because I'll be out of the studio for a few days, but I think I can still make my deadline." I gulped at the word dead and pushed forward. "I know I seem callous but please, when you search there could you be very careful? If you break them..."

He nodded. "I'll put out the word for you."

"Thank you. I don't want you to think I don't realize that this is awful and..."

"I get it. You're a small business owner. There's nothing to fall back on. My dad owns a roofing company and my sister is a landscaper. She threw her back out last summer and was out of work for a couple weeks. I know how the smallest thing can impact a small business. We'll be as careful as we can."

Suddenly, I felt bad for thinking of him as Officer Shorty. He wasn't short, just shorter than the other cop. "What's your name?"

"Officer Langer. One of the detectives will be here soon and she'll run things. I'll make sure I introduce you."

"Thank you," I said. We went outside into the bright November morning. It was a bit too chilly to comfortably sit on the porch.

"We can sit in my car," Micah offered before I could come up with a better solution.

I nodded and followed him to the brown Ford Explorer parked in front of my place. As we were climbing in, a couple more cars pulled up.

"Probably the detective and coroner," Micah said, without my asking.

"Start at the beginning and tell me again," he commanded.

Yes, *commanded*. As if I were his lackey.

I put up with such imperiousness from my father because...well, he was my father. And I knew that despite his sometimes icy exterior, he loved me. But I wasn't about to put up with it from his employee. "Listen, Micah, I appreciate you coming down, but you can tell my father I have it handled. I had to speak to the cops, but I've got no obligation to speak to you."

"You did pay me my retainer, so I am your legit attorney. Tell me again."

I sighed.

I studied Micah... It took me a moment to remember his last name. McCain. Micah McCain.

In other circumstances I might be attracted to him. He wasn't groomed like one of my father's regular associates. His dark black hair was just a bit too long. It hung over his ears a little too far to be a professional haircut. And he had scruff. It looked as if he hadn't shaved in a few days. At that moment, he ran his fingers through his hair and I caught the glimpse of a tattoo on his forearm, though I couldn't make it out.

He wore glasses, but as I studied him, his ice blue eyes looked back at me, studying me.

I sighed and acquiesced, running down my itinerary yesterday again and then stopped. "I really have no clue who did it. I didn't hear anything. The kiln wasn't on when I went to bed."

"Who else has access to your shop?" he asked.

Now that was a good question.

I thought about it before I answered.

"Miss Betty next door comes over a lot. She has keys.

"Adi Zeleski works here a couple days most weeks. Now that the storefront's open, I have her come in if I can't be here during business hours and on Saturdays and sometimes Fridays."

"Anyone else?" he pressed.

"My father. But seriously, can you picture Josiah Lawe, Esquire murdering someone and then cooking them in my kiln? Frankly, I don't know that my father has the first idea how to start a kiln. That's another element to think about. Firing up the kiln. Someone would have to have some know-how."

"That's my next question," Micah said, "but let's stay with people in your studio. Anyone else?"

"My students."

"What students?" he asked.

"My *Wine and Mud* class. We normally meet on Friday nights."

"Who all is in the group?" Micah asked.

For the first time, I noticed he had a small notebook and was writing.

"Barbara Ann Miller, Charlotte Neiman, Julie Iron, Liz Champion, and Helen Smith," I said slowly as he wrote.

I was sure no one in the group could have done it. They were all middle-aged mothers who started the *Wine and Mud* group as a way to get out. Occasionally someone missed because of a conflict, but it was rare. Their fee for using the studio and my instruction was a nice bonus revenue stream. Plus I had two different kids' classes on the weekends. I loved introducing kids to the ceramic arts.

"Tell me about the women," Micah instructed.

"There's nothing to tell. They're mothers." I shrugged. They all had different interests and different lives, but on those Friday nights they came together as mothers looking for a night out. Mothers and amateur potters.

"Harriet, I know you understand that even mothers can murder," Micah said in a very snarky way.

"First, my father named me Harriet after one of his favorite professors. But I've never been Harriet to anyone other than him. It's Harry. Secondly, let's be clear, you don't know that this was a murder. Maybe someone just wanted to cremate a loved one and couldn't afford to."

Micah shot me a look that said he wasn't buying it. Which was hard to be annoyed with since I wasn't buying it either.

"Fine, maybe it's not probable, but it's possible that this isn't murder and there's some other explanation for the corpse in my kiln."

Humph, he snorted.

"You sound just like my father," I said.

"I'll take that as a compliment," he said, almost smiling.

For a moment, that awareness I'd had earlier came back in a flash. If this man ever truly smiled, it would be a sight to see.

"Listen, I appreciate your coming down, but I think I'll be fine. I didn't do anything and I trust the legal system to find out who did do whatever was done." It was a nice speech.

Micah McCain wasn't impressed. "You can't be that naïve. You worked as an attorney before you went all Bohemian and started your business."

"Oh, yes I can," I assured him. "And if being Bohemian is the worst thing you can say about me, I'll take it, though I'd prefer business woman and entrepreneur."

I realized that he'd parroted my father and nothing I could say would convince him that my *little business* was anything other than a lark.

I went back to silence being the best stance.

He was just as silent, which was irksome. After a few minutes of silent standoff, I said, "I will call you if I find myself in need of your services."

"I think I'll stick around until the police clear the scene."

I shrugged. "Whatever."

As if on cue, Officer Shorty— Langer—and a woman came to the car. She was medium. Medium brown hair. Medium height. Not beautiful, but not ugly. Just medium.

The officer knocked on Micah's window. "Miss Lawe, this is Detective Dana."

"Hi," I said inanely. "I hope you have some idea who could have done this."

"We'll do our best to figure it out." She nodded towards a car in the driveway. "I'd like you to come down to the station so we can take your official statement. I can take you down."

"That's all right, Detective. We'll follow you over," I said.

"Your friend doesn't need to come, unless he was here when you found the body."

I shook my head. Micah was right, though I wasn't going to admit that to him. "He wasn't here when I found the body, but he does need to come with me. He's my attorney."

Chapter Two

"I didn't realize that ceramics was so much science and math.
Learning how to fire a piece properly is a key process."
~~Harry's Pottery: A Personal Journey

If Micah McCain said *I told you so*, or even smirked at me, I'd scream.

Lucky for him, he did neither.

Instead, he said with lawyerly firmness, "We'll meet you there, Detective."

Unless they were arresting me, there was nothing for the cops to say to that other than *okay*.

I held my breath for the beat it took the detective to say, "Okay. I'll meet you there."

I let my breath out, but then stuck to my silence offensive as Micah drove the few blocks to Perry Square. He parked the car in one of their new back-in parking spaces around the square. I hated them. I could never back my car back in at the right angle. I never ended up between the painted lines.

I'd spend a crazy amount of time trying and normally only succeeded in making a spectacle of myself.

It was stupid to think about parking when I was about to be interviewed by the police about a murder. But it was easier to think about parking than the bones in my kiln.

When Micah turned off the car, he didn't open the door. Instead he looked at me. "Listen to me and listen good, Harriet. Tell the detective what you know, but if I tell you shut up, then please shut up and let me take over."

I gave him a look and he corrected himself. "*Harry*."

"All I can do is tell them what I know and that's not very much. You weren't there so what can you tell them?"

He sighed. "Just follow my lead. You'll answer all their questions, but carefully. And before you remind me that you're an attorney, let me remind you that one of the things that makes a lawyer effective is that they're removed from the situation. An attorney has perspective that a client never can. You are not removed from this incident. It has impacted you fully. That's why you need me. So keep your answers short and stick to the facts. Don't speculate or draw conclusions. Just the facts as you know them."

He was right. And while he wasn't smirking or saying so, I knew he was feeling all smug about it. Still, I simply said, "Fine."

"And Harry," he said, with more-human less-robot in his voice. "It's going to be okay."

"I don't believe I'm in trouble over this because I didn't do it, so that part is going to be okay. " I planned to continue to repeat this to myself, over and over. It would be okay.

It didn't help.

What happened was finally sinking in. "But someone broke into my studio, burned a body in my kiln. They…"

I shook my head. I wasn't sure how to describe how violated I was feeling. "I don't know if I can ever feel safe there again."

Micah reached across the car, took my hand and said, "As soon as the cops give us permission, I'll help change the locks and maybe add a security camera?"

And suddenly, my father's new attorney didn't seem quite as annoying as he had earlier.

I didn't know anything about security systems and would relish someone else's advice.

I simply said, "Thank you."

I got out of Micah's SUV and stood a moment, staring at Perry Square, trying to calm my racing heart.

I took a deep breath. Autumn leaves were browning on the ground as people bustled around the park, which was the heart of the city. Perry Square made up two city blocks. Trees, a stage, a fountain, and a sitting-wall gave it character.

A statue of Oliver Hazard Perry gave it a firm connection to the city.

All those people walking by were just going about their day, doing whatever it was they were supposed to be doing.

I was *supposed* to be in the studio, working on my for-hire order. I was supposed to be saying "good morning" to occasional shoppers. I was supposed to be going along with my happy routine.

Instead, I was here, getting ready to walk into the police station.

"Are you ready?" Micah asked.

I nodded and followed him across the street to the backside of City Hall, where the door to the police station was.

I'd known it was here, but I'd never been in the police department. I was not a defense attorney. I was a contract attorney. My job had been to keep clients out of potential lawsuits not out of jail.

I suddenly felt my lack of experience profoundly.

I followed Micah down a hall to a door that led to a small box-like room with a glass window between the lobby and the police.

A woman at the desk came up to the glass and spoke through the small hole in it. "Can I help you?"

Before either Micah or I could answer, Detective Dana came to the window. "I'll let you in," she said briskly.

The door next to the glass wall buzzed and then opened. She led us down the hall to a room. There was a long, meeting table, a bunch of chairs, and a camera.

"I'm going to tape this interview," she said. "This is Detective Micci Dana interviewing...say your name," she instructed, looking at me.

"Harriet Lawe," I said on cue.

"And her attorney..."

"Micah McCain," he said.

"Ms. Lawe, please tell me about your day yesterday until the police arrived this morning," the detective instructed.

I looked at Micah and he nodded and quirked his eyebrow as a reminder to keep it short and stick to the facts.

So I did. I went over the same list I gave to Micah. The detective asked about access to the studio and I gave those names out as well.

As I did, I realized that my friends and father were suspects now. They'd be questioning Dad, Miss Betty, Adi, and the women in my class. I felt a stab of guilt, though that was absurd. This was nothing I'd done.

"I don't think anyone on that list would have killed someone, much less stowed the body in my kiln," I said.

"Then how do you propose the body in question got into the kiln? There was no evidence of someone breaking in."

"I..." I paused. "Maybe whoever owned the place before me had a key? I bought it in a short sale. The bank had the keys and it never occurred to me to change the locks. I should have. But whoever owned the place before me, before the bank took it back, could have kept a set."

"And you didn't change the locks?" Micah asked incredulously.

That's right. My *supposed* lawyer, the man who was supposed to be protecting me and representing my interests in this deposition, just called me stupid.

I wanted to be annoyed and have some quick-witted comeback.

The problem was, I had to agree with him. Not changing the locks when I bought the place was a mistake.

I could come up with all kinds of excuses. My life had been in chaos. I'd been going through a divorce and renovations. I'd been contemplating quitting my job...and by contemplating I meant I already knew that I wanted to quit working for my father, but I didn't know how to tell him.

Oh, I could come up with a ton of excuses, but not changing the locks was a mistake.

One that was coming back to haunt me.

Micah shot me a look and I realized he'd said that to offer up alternate suspects to the detective. So maybe it wasn't so stupid after all.

Detective Dana gave Micah a look that said she couldn't believe my attorney had called me stupid either.

I shrugged off his possible insult and decided to offer up those other suspects. "I don't know what to say other than it simply never occurred to me in the midst of the renovations and divorce. Oh, and the contractors all had copies of my keys, too. I got them back when they finished the renovations, but there's no reason to think they couldn't have made copies."

I started to feel sick again. How on earth had I allowed that many people to have access to my studio and house?

Because of that oversight, I had a body in my kiln.

Suddenly, I could see the skeleton again. This time it was staring at me with accusation in its eyes... well, in its glowing eye sockets.

"I—"

I was going to be sick.

"I need a restroom now," I said.

The detective had enough investigative skills to see why I needed the restroom. She ran down the hall and showed me the door.

I managed to make it inside before I started throwing up again.

To be honest, there was nothing much left in my stomach so it was mainly retching. My father would say polite young women didn't speak of retching, but as an officer of the court, even if I wasn't currently practicing law, I found it best to tell the truth.

Retching it was.

I rinsed out my mouth, splashed my face with cold water. The detective was waiting for me in the hall.

"Sorry. I just remembered finding the..." I shuddered and for a moment thought about running back into the bathroom, but managed to get myself back under control.

"I think that's enough for the day," the detective said. She shot me a look that wasn't quite as accusatory. It might have even been a bit sympathetic. "You're not planning to leave town."

It was a statement, not a question. And any thoughts of sympathy from Detective Dana disappeared.

I shook my head.

"If I have any questions, I'll know where to find you," she said.

"Officer Langer said I could get some clothes and my purse from the...crime scene when they finished, but you came first."

The detective nodded. "I'll call down and let them know you're coming for your things."

"Thank you."

We walked back down the hall and he opened the door. "She can go now," she told Micah.

Micah got up, handed the detective his card. "If you need anything else from my client, you can call me and we'll come back down."

I saw the detective's eyes narrow.

"My father is Josiah Lawe," I said. "He sent Micah down. I didn't ask for him to come."

I didn't mention I was an attorney as well. It seemed to me being a poor potter would be more sympathetic than being an attorney. I hadn't practiced very long, but I did notice that attorneys were rarely, if ever, considered sympathetic people.

The detective nodded and I was right, she did look more sympathetic. "I'll call the guys at the crime scene and tell them you're on your way to pick up a few things and I'll be in touch."

"Thank you."

Micah and I were both silent as we walked out to his car. Once we were inside and I'd buckled up again, I said, "Could you drop me off at my place? I need to pick up some clothes and my purse."

"Where are you planning to go? Your father's?"

I didn't snort, but it was a near thing. "I don't think that would be wise. My father and I do very well with Sunday brunch every week. But more than that would be...unwise. I'll just get a room at a hotel until they release the...crime scene."

I knew that there was very little money in my bank account to cover a room, but that's why the gods had invented Visa. I prayed the police had been careful of the greenware. If I got back into the studio in a couple days, I could maybe finish the order in time if I worked nonstop.

I suddenly realized there was a body in my kiln this morning.

I wasn't sure if the cops would take it as evidence, but even if they didn't, I knew I'd never want to fire anything in that kiln again.

I'd have to call and order a new one and then...

I started to put a list together in my head.

It might seem callous, but thinking about practical things was easier than thinking about who killed the skeleton in my kiln.

If they ever made a movie of the week based on my story, that would be a great title. *The Skeleton in My Kiln.*

"Harry?" Micah said.

I pulled myself from my wandering thoughts and said, "Pardon?"

"I said, I have a guestroom you're welcome to use, at least until you can figure out what's next."

His offer surprised me. "You don't know me. What if I *was* the murderer? You'd be inviting me into your home."

"I don't have a kiln at my house, so I suspect I'd be safe."

It took me a moment to realize he was joking. It was a lame joke, but a joke nonetheless.

I smiled as I weighed his offer. I could go to my father's house. I was sure he'd put me up, but the thought of staying with him wasn't tenable. My father and I did much better when we saw each other for one brunch a week.

He loved me. I loved him. But we were very different people.

I could get a hotel room, but money was tight and with my big order in question it could be even tighter.

Miss Betty would probably let me crash there, but I hated to impose.

Micah wasn't a friend I didn't want to take advantage of. He wasn't my father. And he wasn't a hotel.

It wasn't a glowing review, but it would do.

Plus, Micah would probably earn some brownie points from my father for taking me off his hands.

I found myself nodding. "If you're sure, I'll take you up on your offer for the moment. I need to make plans."

Micah nodded. "I'm sure. And it's a good time to assure you that I never say anything I don't mean."

Chapter Three

"Every time I open the kiln, I hold my breath.
I'm just waiting to see what surprises it holds."
~Harry's Pottery: A Personal Journey

I thought Micah's home would be an apartment or house, not a *home*. I thought it would be something sleek, sterile, and lawyerly.

Instead, his home surprised me. He lived in a modest east Erie neighborhood in a small, brick house with a huge maple tree in the front. The branches were bare now, but I could imagine the shade it would cast over the house in the summer.

There was a big front porch with bulky wooden furniture and a bright red door with a brass knocker.

He opened the door and the surprises continued. Hardwood floors, an antique coat tree, an overstuffed leather sofa in front of the front window, and shelves and shelves filled with books.

There was a cross-stitched wall hanging of Blind Justice, with something written on it. I moved close enough to read it. "*Rightful liberty is unobstructed action according to our will within limits drawn around us by the equal rights of others. I do not add 'within the limits of the law' because law is often but the tyrant's will, and always so when it violates the rights of the individual.* Thomas Jefferson."

"This is lovely," I said. There were initials in the corner. MMM. I pointed and looked at him.

"My grandmother made it for my father when he started law school. Maggie Mae McCain. He gave it to me when I passed the bar. If I followed tradition, it would hang in my office, but I think it looks at home here."

I nodded. Home. Yes, that's exactly what Micah's place looked like.

"It does," I said.

He grabbed my bag and led me up the stairs and opened a door to the left. He set my bag down and said, "You're welcome to stay as long as you need to. I'm gone more than I'm here. The bathroom's across the hall. The kitchen's pretty well stocked." He glanced at his watch. "I've got to get back to the office, but I'll grab some takeout for dinner on the way home. There's a spare key I'll leave in the bowl on the hall table in case you need to go out."

"Thanks. I'm grateful to have a moment to figure out what's next."

"No problem." He turned to go back down the stairs, then turned back.

"You should call your father. He was worried."

I nodded. "I will. Thanks again, Micah."

He was already gone.

I sat on the edge of the quilt-covered, four-poster bed that was dark with age. Nothing in this house matched my first impression of my father's firm's newest attorney.

Remembering my promise, I dialed my father. It went to voicemail, which probably meant he was still in court. "Hi, it's me. I'm fine. Thanks for sending Micah. It wasn't necessary, but it was good to have someone there with me. I can't get back into my house for a while since it's a crime scene. Micah set me up at his place. Uh. Well, that's it. There's nothing to worry about."

Next I called Miss Betty. She'd seen the commotion next door, but all she said about it was, "Is there anything I can do, dear?"

I was so thankful. I wasn't sure how to explain a dead body in my kiln, because frankly, I didn't understand it myself.

"I'll tell you all about it in person tomorrow or the next day. I just wanted to let you know that I can't take you to the store today. I'll call Barnabas and see if he'll run you over."

"It's not every day a handsome man takes me out," Miss Betty quipped. "But you don't need to worry about me. I'll call him myself."

I sighed…one item off my very long list. "Thanks."

"Remember, you have friends here," she said.

"Thank you," I said again for lack of anything else to say. I hung up and felt teary.

My cheeks felt cool. I reached up and felt tears rolling down my face. I realized I was crying. Soon, it was more than tears. My chest heaved as I sobbed. The shock of finding a skeleton in my kiln was hitting me.

I couldn't seem to stop shaking and crying.

It was ridiculous, I kept telling myself. I didn't carry on like this when my mother passed away.

But this morning, before I'd come downstairs, I'd been happy.

I'd been living life on my own terms.

And now?

Now my house and studio were filled with police and there was a dead body in my kiln.

Suddenly, Micah was in the open doorway.

Without saying a word, he sat next to me on the bed and put an arm around me.

"It's okay," he crooned over and over.

And slowly, his words penetrated and my sobbing slowed down.

But even then, he continued to hold me.

***

I opened my very crusty eyes and looked around an unfamiliar room. In that split second of opening my eyes, my morning came rushing back to me. I sat up and realized I'd been covered up with a quilt. As I kicked it off, something rustled and I realized it was a note.

Had two appointments I couldn't miss. I'll be back asap. Make yourself at home. Fridge is stocked. Help yourself. M.

He'd said that before, but after my little meltdown, he probably was afraid I wouldn't remember.

I looked at the clock. It was two p.m.

I tried to decide how long I'd been out and couldn't. Hours for sure.

My stomach growled, reminding me that I hadn't eaten.

I grabbed my phone and found six messages on it.

One was from my father. One from Barnabas. One from my other neighbors, Hap and Kitty Meyers. One from my employee, Adi Zeleski. One from one of my *Wine and Mud* class students, Julie Iron. There was an unknown number on the phone with a message attached. It was a woman who introduced herself as Emm Kline from the news.

I knew I couldn't handle any of the calls until I had something in my stomach. I went downstairs, through the living room and dining room to Micah's kitchen. Here was another room that I would never have guessed belonged to him.

One entire wall was filled with cast iron cookware. Frying pans of all sizes. Griddles. Biscuit pans.

There was a white Kitchen-Aide Mixer in the corner.

It looked as if Micah was a cook.

I was not.

My idea of cooking was eating out. And if forced to produce food for myself at home, I was all about microwaving. I could microwave frozen dinners and leftovers from restaurants. If I were feeling wild, I'd try eggs.

I opened Micah's ginormous refrigerator. It was as neat and tidy as the kitchen. A bowl in the front had some kind of pasta in it. Feeling a bit guilty, but knowing I'd be able to think better with food in my stomach, I took him at his word and helped myself.

I microwaved a plate of the pasta and at the first bite I knew that if Micah ever followed my footsteps and left the legal world behind, he should pursue cooking professionally.

There were cherry tomatoes, fresh basil, and a lot of garlic, without being overwhelming. I took another bite. Cheese. Some light sauce that pulled it all together.

For a few moments, I forgot about my morning. I forgot I was virtually homeless until the police released my studio and apartment. I forgot the calls I needed to return and simply savored the delicious pasta.

I was just taking the last bite when Micah walked into the kitchen. "I was hoping you ate. I thought about bringing home take-out, but instead I stopped at the store and got ingredients for dinner."

"I really should go..." I started but stopped as he shook his head.

"I've got the extra room. I made some calls and you should be able to get back into your place tomorrow or the following day at the latest. The cops didn't find anything. No point of entry and no indication that you had anything to do with it.

But since there's no evidence that anyone broke in, we're back to looking at people who have keys."

"And since I never changed the locks when I bought the place, I've complicated things. I know who's had access to my keys, but I have no clue who might have had them a few years ago. Trisha Something-Or-Other owned the building. I can get her name from the neighbors and I'm sure the cops can track her down."

"I'll let them know." He started to unpack his reusable grocery bag. "So, are you staying?"

I watched as ingredients lined his counter. "I thought something comfort food-ish was called for. Meatloaf, mashed potatoes, and breaded cauliflower. I bought ice cream for dessert, since I don't really have time to make something more elaborate."

I almost swooned. A man who cooked and brought home ice cream?

He was a winner in my book.

"I got Triple Chocolate and Pecan Pralines."

Yes. Micah McCain was a true renaissance man.

"If you're sure," I said, mouth-watering hunger outweighing awkwardness. The pasta was just an appetizer.

58

"I'm sure." He looked me over assessing me. It might have felt intrusive from someone else, but I could see the concern in his eyes, so it didn't. "Listen, why don't you go up and take a long bath. Millie has a cornucopia of bath salts and stuff in the hall bathroom. Help yourself to whatever you want. Take your time. I'll start dinner and make a few more calls. We'll get you home as soon as possible."

Millie. His girlfriend? An ex who happened to leave bath stuff around? A friend with benefits?

At any other time, I might have felt inclined to ask, but right now I just felt numb so I simply mumbled, "Thank you."

"Oh, and I talked to Officer Langer. I was supposed to tell you that the police were very careful with the pieces you said were delicate. They had to check them all out and can't guarantee that everything went back where they got it from, but nothing broke."

I breathed a huge sigh of relief. That was one worry that hadn't really been registering but was a relief to put it to rest. "Oh, that's good. It's part of a production order and being out of the studio for a few days is going to put me behind enough. If they broke inventory I don't know if I could have caught up."

"I'm glad then."

"Me, too." The thought of a bath was enticing. "And thanks for the offer. I think I'd like to get out of these clothes."

That sounded suggestive, so I stammered, "I didn't mean, I mean, I..." I stopped myself. "You know what I meant."

Micah chuckled and said, "I do. Go. I'll get started."

Micah's bathroom was equipped with one of the biggest claw foot tubs I'd ever seen. And his possible girlfriend had an impressive collection of high-end bath products. I picked a lemon and lavender bath-bomb.

I looked in the mirror and understood why Micah had looked so sympathetic after his once over. I was never bronzed by any sense of the word. In fact, if asked to describe my complexion most days I'd say neon white. But today, it was translucent white, which only emphasized my freckles. And my hair...well, it was reddish enough to stand out on a good hair-day, but today was not a good hair-day. My impromptu nap in Micah's guestroom has loosened my Medusa hair from its twisty and little red wisps stuck in various directions.

I groaned and sank into the tub.

I loved my apartment, but it had a decidedly apartment-sized tub. When I took a bath there were...well, islands.

Now, I'm sure some women are endowed to the extent that *islands* are a way of life when they bathe. I was not endowed. Back in school, my friend Lou used to tease me that I was concave.

I wasn't, but it was a near thing.

So, having islands was more a reflection on my tub than on my anatomy.

I did not have any islands in Micah's massive tub. As a matter of fact, the water covered me from my toes to my shoulders.

The bath-bomb smelled heavenly and for the first time, I felt that I'd managed to wash the stench of burned-up-person off me.

And suddenly, I was back in my kiln room, peering in the kiln and seeing a skull. I started to shake and felt another wave of nausea.

I dunked my head under the water, wanting to be sure any dead body odor was gone.

I came back up for air and was disgusted with myself. This wasn't me.

I was a strong, decisive woman.

When Alex said he was leaving me, I didn't curl up in a ball and whimper. I took a look at my life, decided what would make me happy, and then made it happen.

Someone was trying to ruin that hard-won happiness.

Someone had broken into my studio and put a body in my kiln.

Here I was cowering. Letting Micah take over.

I was done with that.

I got out of the tub, got dressed and threw my wet medusa hair in a messy bun. I'd welcomed the messy bun coming into style since that was my hair's status quo.

I was going to accept Micah's offer to spend the night because frankly, I didn't want to waste money on a hotel and my other option was staying at my father's. Micah was the lesser of two evils. But I was going to set firm boundaries. I appreciated his help today while I suffered through my momentary weakness, but I was fine. I could handle things myself. I was going to be clear and to the point.

I started down the stairs and smelled dinner.

I'd be clear and to the point after I ate.

Then I heard voices and groaned. I recognized both.

One was Micah's and one was...my father's.

I squared my shoulders and continued down the stairs.

After a traumatic event, some people's parents would rush to them and sweep them into a hug, needing to be sure they were all right.

My father looked me up and down, gave me a brisk nod and said, "You know you're welcome to stay at my house."

"Thank you, but since Micah's representing me, it's good to be here in case the police want to talk to me again."

He nodded. "Micah said you have no idea who might have done this?"

It was a question, not a statement. He was questioning how his daughter could let someone get burned up in her kiln without having a clue who'd done it.

"I don't have a clue," I said firmly. "But one way or another, I'll figure out who tried to ruin my business and implicate me in...whatever this is."

Maybe the body in the kiln had nothing to do with me?

It could be a murderer trying to cover their tracks. I have to think burning a body takes care of a lot of trace evidence.

"What do you think someone's motive might be?" my father asked.

"There's not enough evidence yet to say. All I can say for sure is there was a skeleton in my kiln and I didn't put it there," I told him. My father was a man who appreciated facts.

"Micah said you really don't know how many people had access to keys." There was censure in his voice.

"Micah obviously has said a lot," I said slowly, glaring at him. "But he's right, I don't know."

My father spoke as if he were speaking to a client, slowly and deliberately. "That was ill advised."

I sighed. "Yes, yes it was."

"You're sure you don't want to come stay at my house?" he asked.

"I'm fine. It's just for one night and I'm already settled here."

My father stood up and nodded. "I've got court tomorrow and need to get home to prepare. You're in good hands with Micah."

"I'm in good hands with myself," I said and realized how juvenile it sounded. I wished I could suck the words back in.

"You are," he said. He gave me a long look and then nodded ever so slightly, as if confirming he'd expected whatever he saw. "I'm glad you're all right."

"Thank you."

"I'll see myself out," he said to Micah.

I heard the front door close and Micah busied himself stirring something on the stove.

When he finally turned around, he said, "I'm sorry."

"For?" I asked.

"Obviously, you didn't want me telling your father anything. I'm used to discussing cases with him and he is your father, so it didn't occur to me you'd object, but I was wrong. It was a breach of my privilege and I apologize."

I sighed again. Sighing was something I did a lot when my father was around. "No, it wasn't a breach of attorney-client privilege. I would have told him, and if you'd asked me, I would have told you to tell him. My father and I simply don't get along. It's not even really that. We're simply awkward together. I'd hoped when I worked at the firm, we'd get closer—that we'd find some common ground. We did fine as long as we were talking about clients, but anything beyond that never got more comfortable."

I shrugged and tried to look nonchalant. "It is what it is."

"He came here as soon as he got out of court because he was worried about you."

"He was worried about how it would look if his daughter was charged with...whatever this is. He's hoped the legal world would forget he had a daughter who stopped practicing law and started playing with clay for a living."

That's how he'd put it. *Playing with clay.*

It had hurt then.

It still hurt now.

I don't think he meant it the way I took it, but that didn't make it sting less.

"I don't think you're being fair to him," Micah said softly.

"I'm sure you don't. Do you have family?"

"My parents and my sister. Both sets of grandparents and dozens of aunts, uncles, and cousins."

Wow. It was just me and my father. No aunts, uncles, cousins or grandparents around. "That must be nice."

He chuckled. "That's one word for it. *Chaos* is another. They're very loud. We meet at my parent's camp every summer. Everyone. There has to be more than a hundred, when you count my cousins' kids and all the extras that we sort of adopt. Everyone brings tents and RV's. The field is packed. And meals? You have to be very, very quick if you want food."

I could picture it. Gaggles of people with a shared heritage, shared stories, and a shared history.

"I never met either set of grandparents, and both my parents were only children."

He shot me a look of pity.

Rather than feeling comforted by it, I bristled. I changed the subject. "I have a million things to do. My phone is filled with messages. So, if you don't mind, I'm going to start calling people back until dinner. Then tomorrow, I'm going to have to do a million errands."

"Like what?" he asked.

"I need to go buy a new kiln first off. Whether or not they keep that one as evidence doesn't matter. I can't imagine using it again."

He nodded. "I see your point. It's about a half hour until dinner."

Despite the fact I'd just eaten, that sounded wonderful. "Great, I'll get started."

Chapter Four

"A potter gets very attached to their tools. We are creatures of habit."
~Harry's Pottery: A Personal Journey

The next day, Micah dropped me at my place and I got my car.

I drove to neighboring Corry where I ordered a new kiln from M & M Pottery. They'd had an order canceled and had a kiln in stock. They promised to deliver it by next week, maybe as soon as Monday. I was driving back to Erie when Micah called to say the police had released my house.

He offered to call a locksmith he knew, but I declined. I was standing on my own two feet. I called a locksmith, who promised to meet me at my place after two.

Then I picked up my suitcase at Micah's. As I dropped his spare key in the bowl, I realized it would have been just that easy. Someone could borrow someone else's key, make a copy and return it without the owner being any the wiser. I'd like to think a total stranger broke in, but I had to allow that anyone who'd ever used my key could be the one

It was a sobering thought.

I drove home and pulled in the drive that led to the garage in the back, as well as the six parking spaces for shoppers.

I locked my car securely in the garage and went inside through the back door. I had the option of walking up the back stairs to my apartment, or through a door to the studio.

I put my overnight bag down and went into the studio.

I could tell that the police had searched, but they'd been respectful and neat. I was relieved when I examined the shelves in the kiln room. They were full and as near as I could tell, nothing was broken.

The kiln was still in the room.

I nervously moved around a plate on the shelf, looking at the kiln with my peripheral vision. I was supposed to load this greenware into the kiln yesterday. But everything had changed when I came downstairs.

It was hard to believe it was only a day ago.

In just a little over twenty-four hours and everything had changed through no fault of my own.

That's what happened when Alex decided he wasn't happy...change. In retrospect, even though I hadn't started it, I was happy with how things turned out.

But try as I might, I couldn't imagine ever being happy now that I found a body in my kiln.

Someone had altered my life and that thought made me mad.

Last night, I'd had tons of calls about the body. Neighbors and customers, some calling with a pretext, some boldly asking what had happened. A couple seemed to feel as if I might admit I'd killed someone.

I'd only talked to true friends. But I couldn't avoid the rest of the world for long.

Whoever had done this had changed my life in ways I didn't like.

And I suspected that I'd be under suspicion—not by just the police but by the public—until the real killer was found.

I sighed.

I felt bewildered and befuddled.

I didn't like either feeling.

I decided that I'd be proactive and see if Barnabas would give me a hand moving the dead-body kiln out of the studio in preparation for the new one arriving.

He didn't pick up his phone, so I hung up, went back to the shed and got out the Dollie.

Maybe I could move it myself.

There was no way I was sleeping in a building that had a dead-body kiln in it.

On the heels of that thought came the next one...I'd already slept in a house with a dead-body kiln.

And on the heels of that thought came the realization that I'd slept in a house with a potential murderer or at least an illegal burner of bodies in it.

As I finished with all those heels of thoughts, I got a rampant case of the heebie-jeebies.

But I got the Dollie under the kiln, strapped the kiln in place, and eased it out of the kiln room with care.

I wheeled it out through the storefront because the back stairs were steeper than the front stairs.

I opened the door and found Detective Dana on my porch.

"Harriet we'd like you to come down to the station and answer a few more questions." She nodded at the kiln on the Dollie. "Where were you going with that?"

"I was hoping my neighbor would help me get it down the stairs so I can store it in the shed until I figure out what to do with it."

She continued looking at me with questioning expression.

Being able to talk without saying anything had to be a handy skill for a detective, I inanely thought.

"I can't go to sleep tonight with a dead-body kiln in the house," I said.

"Okay," she said slowly as if my veracity was in doubt. "Could you leave it there and come back to the station with me?"

"I'd rather talk here. I'm waiting for a locksmith."

Again, she gave me a look that said more than words could, so I went ahead and answered her unasked question. "We've established I don't know who has keys. I can't stay here not knowing who has access to my place. Especially since knowing that the someone who does have access tried to burn a corpse in the kiln."

She stepped inside, obviously having decided to ask me whatever she wanted to ask me here. "Do you know a Steve Summers?"

I thought about it but couldn't come up with anything. "I don't think so."

She opened her phone and showed me a picture.

The picture a blast from the past and it was easy to know exactly when the picture was taken. I was wearing a frothy pink dress that was a giveaway. "That's me at my prom. I have a reunion next year…I still can't believe it."

She ignored that and pointed to the picture. "And who is that you're dancing with?"

"Junior..." and suddenly I knew. "Junior Summers. Why?"

"Junior was actually Steve Summers, Jr. Aaaaaand..." She was eyeing me uncomfortably as she let that *And* draw out an exceptionally long time. "he's the body from your kiln."

I hadn't seen Junior since graduation. I hadn't even seen him at a reunion. And yet, his body had been in this very kiln.

"Would you care to explain?"

"I think I'd like to call my lawyer," I said.

She nodded and said, "And I think we should probably finish this at the station."

***

I called Micah, who met me at the station. I also called Miss Betty and asked her to wait for the locksmith.

Detective Dana insisted I ride to the station with her.

She had an unmarked car, so I wasn't in the back of a police car, but it was odd riding in the back while she drove.

I declined to answer any of Detective Dana's questions until Micah arrived. But I knew that when I did answer them, there wouldn't be much to say. Junior Summers and I hadn't been friends in high school. We ran with different circles. I was a geek. He was a druggie. Everyone in the school knew Junior was who you went to see if you wanted something. Everyone—even a few adults.

I'd danced with him at prom because I'd danced with anyone who asked. Even if I didn't like them. I never saw the point in hurting someone's feelings. Especially when a dance only lasted a few minutes. I could handle anything for a few minutes.

"When was the last time you saw Steve Summers?"

"Maybe at our five-year reunion? I didn't go to the ten." It was more of a question than answer. "I don't remember talking to him. I don't even remember if he was there. But that would be my best guess. If he wasn't there, then graduation day."

I paused. Suddenly remembering that last time vividly.

"Wait. The last time I remember seeing Junior was out in the parking lot after graduation. After the ceremony. My father and I walked by Junior and his family. They looked angry. And suddenly his dad reached out and smacked him. Hard. Across the cheek. My father was furious, not that anyone who didn't know him would notice. My father is very self-contained. But that day he strode over to Junior and asked if he needed somewhere to go."

"Did Summers go with you and your father?" the detective asked.

"No. He said he was fine, but I don't think he was." I was suddenly back all those years ago. I remember the look on Steve's face. He hadn't been relieved we'd stopped or that my father had offered help. He'd been furious.

"That sounds convenient," Detective Dana said derisively.

"Sometimes that's how life is...convenient. And sometimes it's not convenient at all—like when you find a body in your kiln. Now, if you don't mind, I'd like to get back to my place and get those new locks on and that death kiln out."

"I have more questions," Detective Dana said.

"Ma'am, with all due respect, I've answered all your questions," I said. She seemed to ruffle at my calling her ma'am. I got that. I'd reached an age where I occasionally got ma'amed and I never liked it.

I ignored the *ma'am-ruffle* and continued, "Yes, I knew Junior in school. No, I don't know him now. And I have no idea how he ended up in my kiln. So, unless you're arresting me, I'm leaving. If you have any further questions, please contact Micah."

I stood and walked to the door, holding my breath. Would she arrest me? I didn't think she could have enough to arrest me, but maybe...

I opened the door and turned down the hall, Micah on my heels.

As we walked into the parking lot, I finally let out a long breath.

"Wow," he said.

"I was over it. This is a nightmare not of my own making. I don't know what's going on and who put Junior's body in my kiln, but I'm going to find out." That last sentence was me muttering under my breath. I should probably have kept it just in my head.

"Pardon?" Micah said.

I could have brushed it off, but I was getting tired of this whole thing so I said, "I'm not going to play defense here. I'm going on the offense. I'm going to figure out who put a body in my kiln."

I had thought about asking Micah for a ride home, but I needed to walk this off and I needed to think. "I'll talk to you later."

"As your attorney I feel I should warn you to let the police do their jobs," he said.

"As your client, I will thank you for your concern and talk to you soon." There. I put him in his place. Micah was nice enough. And under normal circumstances, I might even let myself be attracted to him. But these weren't normal circumstances. I needed to stand on my own two feet.

I started across Perry Square Park toward State Street. As I walked down State I could see the bay and the huge tower at the end of the dock.

Office buildings and shops lined the streets.

People walked along, going about their day with no thoughts of kilns and skeletons and going to jail.

I walked by one large building with a sign listing the occupants. The Mac Practice one read.

Mac. That name rang a bell.

Front Street was the second to last turn on State. The only thing closer to the bay was the Bayfront Highway. As I walked along, I wondered why the name Mac was niggling at me.

I didn't use any of the physicians there.

But I did recall reading about someone in that family. It hit me. The Mac

I'd read about was a maid from Erie who lived in LA and cleaned a murder scene.

It was a murky recollection at best.

I hurried towards home, anxious to look her up.

Miss Betty was at my place watching a man working on a handle of the front door.

"Hi, sweetie," she said. "This is Justin. He's already put new locks on the back and other front door to your apartment."

He turned and smiled. "I'm almost finished."

"Thank you so much for putting a rush on this. I don't think I could have slept tonight without it," I said.

He finished up, I paid the invoice, and he handed me the new keys.

Keys I wouldn't be sharing with anyone but my father.

After he left Miss Betty said, "Are you okay?"

For a moment, I wanted to say *yes*. Or *of course*. But Miss Betty wasn't just an elderly neighbor, she was a friend. And a friend deserved better than some pat answer. "No, not really. But once they find who broke into my place, I'll be a bit closer to all right."

Saying break-in was easier than saying murder.

"You're welcome to stay at my place, honey," Miss Betty offered.

I kissed her weathered cheek. "You are truly a very good friend. And I appreciate that, but I'm not letting someone chase me out of my home." Just like I wasn't going to let myself rely on anyone else. I was going to handle this.

I paused and asked, "Do you remember some story about an Erie woman in LA solving some mystery?"

Who needed the internet when they had access to Miss Betty?

She smiled. "Of course, I do. Quincy. That was her name. Quincy Mac. Her family has a medical practice here in town. But Quincy's not a doctor. She solved her first murder...oh, more than a decade ago. She writes now."

"Writes what?" I asked.

"Shows for Hollywood. I'll confess, I watch them all. She did a movie based on that first murder she cleaned. What was the name...?" Miss Betty paused then said, "*Steamed*. She won a Mortie for it. She did some more movies and had been doing a series for HeartMark Channel. I loved *Cereal Killers*."

Miss Betty continued her girl-from-Erie-makes-good-in-LA monologue for a while longer then headed home, but not without hugging me first. "If you need me, just call."

"Thanks, I will," I promised.

She stopped a moment and smiled. "It will be okay."

"I hope so." I wished I felt as confident about that as Miss Betty did.

After she walked next door, I Googled *Quincy Mac.*

My neighbor was very good. She'd hit the high points. Quincy had solve three murders. Three. The first one she accidentally cleaned. The second was someone inspired by that first murder. And the third was much more recent and involved a dead-dead zombie. I laughed when I watched her interview with Stephen Colbert on YouTube. She emphasized the zombies were inherently dead and thus the one she literally tripped over was a dead-dead one and they picked up an old conversation about *Murder She Wrote* that cracked me up.

From what I read, that first murder she accidentally cleaned in *Steamed* led to her finding an entirely new passion with her writing.

I'd already found my passion with pottery and wasn't interested in finding any other new passions. I needed to figure out who broke into my place to burn a body in order to protect the life I'd built.

I was an attorney. I wasn't a trial lawyer, though I'd handled a few cases. I'd spent most of my time lawyering with contracts. But here's the thing. Contracts had to be laid out in a logical way. From point A to point Z to...

An attorney working on a contract had to think of what sort of ramifications each word might have. What sort of implications. How it could impact a client.

I could take that sort of analytical sense and apply it to this. I could figure this out.

Quincy Mac hadn't wanted to go to jail for accidentally cleaning a murder scene and I didn't want to go to jail because someone tried to use my kiln as a crematory.

I was going to Quincy-Mac things.

Yes, I changed her name into an action.

I was going to Quincy-Mac my way out of this.

I was going to find out who put Junior in my kiln.

I wasn't going to wait for the cops to figure things out and rescue me.

I was going to rescue myself.

Chapter Five

"Pottery is about process.
Once you figure out the basics of that
process the real artistry kicks in."
~Harry's Pottery

WWQD.

What would Quincy do?

I wrote that down on a neon pink Post-It note and stuck it to my wall.

Quincy had used a white-board. I was using my idea wall.

One entire wall of my studio was chalkboard painted. I could sketch ideas there, or tape them...or Post-It them.

I sectioned off a corner and wrote down questions with a chalk pen.

Who'd had a key to my studio?

Why would they use a kiln to get rid of a body?

Who had enough knowledge to start the kiln, but not enough knowledge to account for ramping, the slow building of temperature that was part of the firing process?

Who wanted Steve Summers, aka Junior, dead?

And why would they risk bringing him into my studio to cremate him?

I sat down at my wheel, which faced that wall and started to work on my production order.

M&M Pottery had promised to deliver the new kiln soon.

I still had the old kiln sitting on the Dollie.

I'd called Barnabas again later tonight and ask him to help me move it.

I didn't flip my closed sign over to *open*. I needed the quiet, not that I expected many people wanted to shop at a pottery store where someone had been murdered.

I sighed and stared at my board.

Suspects.

I needed suspects.

I was mulling that over when someone knocked on the back door. If it had been the front, I'd have assumed it was a customer, but the back door meant friends.

I walked back and found Barnabas smiling at me.

I opened the door and before I could say hello found myself enveloped in a hug.

Not just any hug.

A bear hug because Barnabas was a bear of a man. Way over six foot, built like a linebacker. He wore his hair shaved close, had a full beard with the faintest hint of grey beginning to show through and a dark honey colored complexion that always made me feel anemic by comparison.

"Lady Bug, you sure enough done did it now," he murmured, using his nickname for me. I'd had a lady bug on my shoulder when we met and the name had stuck. He hugged me tight.

As he released me, I said, "Thanks, I needed that."

"Tell me all about it," he said.

It might have sounded like a command coming from anyone else, but coming from Barnabas, is sounded like concern.

So I told him.

Barnabas glanced at my idea wall and then back at me

I tried to explain, "I read about Quincy Mac. She's from Erie and solved a murder on her own in LA. I'm not sure I'm looking to solve it. I'm just trying to see if I can find anything to help the detectives solve it. I'm going to start with the keys and go from there."

He quirked his massive eyebrow. "Keys?"

"I'm planning to list everyone who has a key to my place. I think figuring this out might be like writing a contract or making a piece of pottery for that matter. It's all about going step-by-step."

"Well, you best put my name and Miss Betty's on your list."

I shook my head. "You two aren't suspects, so I'm not putting your names down."

"Lady Bug have you seen me? I could lift a body into your kiln quick as a New York minute. You'd have to take that into consideration. Someone big enough to do it. I think you and Miss Betty would be hard pressed to lift dead weight into a kiln."

Dead weight. I don't think he intended the sort of pun he'd made and I'm positive he didn't intend to make me shudder, but he had, and I did.

"I'm not putting your name down," I said maintained.

Barnabas laughed as he walked over to my wall and wrote his own name. And Miss Betty's.

I didn't go erase them. He was right. Everyone needed to be listed, but I'd cross off names as I saw fit.

"And I'm going to say I told you so," Barnabas said.

"Told me what?"

"I told you that you needed a dog. Nana Vancy's having another Everything But a Dog day in a couple weeks. I think you should go and look around."

"I don't know if I can manage a dog."

He just shook his head. "Can you manage finding more dead bodies in your studio? Even if it's a little bit of a dog, it would have yapped and let you know someone was here. Maybe even scared them away."

Yapping would have helped. "You do have a point."

"And you happen to know this vet who will go with you and make sure you get a good dog, not that you'd need me if Nana Vancy's around," he added with a grin.

"Why? What's with this woman?" I asked.

"She is a dog matchmaker," he said. "Well, not matching dogs to other dogs, but rather dogs to their people. It's truly amazing. She just gets a feeling and it's a match."

I must have looked skeptical because Barnabas laughed. "You don't think it's a thing until she does it. Her grandson told me she tried her hand at matchmaking people. Those matches stuck too, but she put the couple in question through hell first so the family's just as happy she runs her dog foundation."

"I might just go with you to meet her...not necessarily looking for a dog," I said.

He shrugged. "She reminds me of my mom. She just sweeps you along in the direction she wants you to go." He paused and said, "Speaking of my mom, she said not to cook because she's bringing dinner in a half hour or so."

He was right. Miss Lonnie was a force of nature. She lived in one of the less desirable neighborhoods in town, but her block was spic and span with not a problem in the world because everyone knew and respected Miss Lonnie.

"I was going to call you and ask you to help me get the dead body kiln out of here. Do you think we could do it now before your mom comes?" I asked.

"There's no *we* about it," Barnabas said with a laugh. "I've got it."

And he did.

He jockeyed that Dollie down the stairs and into the garage out back as if it weighed next to nothing.

"Thanks. I don't think I could have slept with that in the house," I started when he came back inside. On his heels, my other neighbors came in… Miss Betty, and Hap and Kitty Meyers.

"Oh, Harry," Kitty said, starting to tear up. "What a trauma. What can we do?"

Barnabas point to the wall. "She's trying to write down everyone who has a key's name. I put mine down because she refused to consider me a suspect."

"I saw everyone coming over, so I came back," Miss Betty said. "And put my name down on your list."

"I already added you," Barnabas said.

"And us," said Hap.

Before I could protest, Barnabas added Hap and Kitty.

I realized that not putting down my friends' names didn't make them less of a suspect in the detective's eyes. Still seeing their names there felt odd.

Frankly, everything had felt odd since I found Junior.

"Did anyone see anything the night of the murder?" Barnabas—chalk pen in hand—asked.

"We don't know it was murder," I protested. "Though they did figure out who it was."

"Oh, that's great news," said Miss Betty.

I shook my head. "It would be...except I went to school with him. Steve Summers, Junior. We just called him Junior back then. I didn't know him well, but I did know him. The detective has a picture of us dancing at the prom."

They all started buzzing, outraged that I was a suspect.

At that moment Miss Lonnie came into the house with a huge casserole dish. She didn't knock. That wasn't unusual. "Make yourself useful, Barnabas. There's more food in the car. Enough for everyone," she said in such a way that I knew that I wasn't going to be alone this evening. "Let's take this up to your kitchen, sweetie."

Soon, we were all eating and occasionally someone would go add a name to a Post-It that was destined for my idea wall.

No one had seen anything unusual, though none of us were night owls.

At that moment, the doorbell for my apartment rang. "Want me to get it?" Barnabas asked.

I nodded.

"Humph." He stomped down the front stairs. Moments later he was back with Micah and my father in tow. "Mama Lonnie, we've got more guests for dinner," Barnabas bellowed.

"What is going on?" my father asked me.

"Just my friends checking in on me," I said.

My father looked a little lost. And I realized that my father had colleagues and employees. He had casual acquaintances and business contacts. He had clients and neighbors. But if asked, I'd be hard pressed to name someone who was my father's friend.

And that struck me as very sad.

"Let me introduce you," I said. "Everyone this is my father and my lawyer, Josiah Lawe and Micah McCain. Dad and Micah, this is..."

And I ran through the list.

Micah was quickly pulled aside by Barnabas, and my father—who had a deer-in-the-headlights look about him—was suddenly filling a plate of food with Lonnie.

Barnabas's mom said something and Dad burst out laughing.

I couldn't remember the last time my father had laughed.

And again, that struck me as sad.

I resolved to do better.

I tried to remember the last time I saw my father truly happy.

We'd gone to a Presque Isle beach after spending the day at Waldemeer. Dad had stopped to get us all ice cream cones and after eating all his ice cream, he tossed the cone towards a group of gulls. One, tried to lift the entire cone, only to have it fall. He dove back onto it before the other birds to grab it and tried again.

Four times that bird tried and failed.

The fifth time, he succeeded.

My father had laughed and said, "He never realized that cone was too big for him. I admire that."

Mom and I finished eating our cones, and the three of us sat together on that rocky beach watching the sunset.

I hadn't thought about that day in years.

I looked at my father and Lonnie and realized that he looked more comfortable with Barnabas's mom than me.

I was going to try to change that.

"Penny for your thoughts," Micah said from behind me. He had a plate loaded with food. "Your friend's mother is an amazing cook."

"Coming from someone who also has amazing cooking skills, that's a huge compliment. You should tell her."

"I will." But he made no move to leave my side. "You have some very nice friends."

"I do. Front Street is very much a community. A small town in the heart of a big city."

Micah quirked his eyebrows and I laughed. "Okay, Erie's not quite a big city, but it's a biggish city."

"Better." He took a bite of casserole, chewed it thoughtfully and asked, "Are you okay after today?"

"I'm okay-ish," I said. "Having my friends show up helped."

"Are you going to be okay sleeping here tonight?"

The kiln was gone. The locks were changed. Still...

I shrugged. "I think so."

"I brought new doorbells. One for each front door. I'm not great at things, but the guy at the store said they were easy to set up. They link to your phone and you can see people at the door, talk to them even."

"I'm not sure whoever brought that body in here rang the doorbell," I pointed out.

"I also bought a spotlight for the back that does the same sort of thing. It's motion activated and you can see whoever tripped it. I'm not sure I can set that up at night, but I'll come by tomorrow and try."

"Micah, I might not have been a trial lawyer, but I'm pretty sure wiring security systems isn't part of an attorney's job description," I said.

"It's a service I provide for very special clients."

I laughed and felt my cheeks warm. Out of the corner of my eye I saw my father's head jerk in my direction.

Micah was flirting with me and I didn't mind it.

It had been a long time since I flirted...or at least been flirted at.

But having my father watch me try to flirt back was more than I could manage.

"My father's looking at us. We'd best mingle," I said.

"Why?" he asked.

I didn't have an answer for him. I just knew that my father was giving us an assessing look that made me nervous.

"Because I want you to meet my friends," I finally said. "Come over and tell Miss Lonnie how good her food is."

That wasn't quite the truth, but it was near enough for now.

What had started as a bad day had ended up in a nice gathering.

After they ate, Barnabas and Micah wired the doorbells. Barnabas promised to come help install the spotlight the next day.

"I don't like you staying here tonight without it hooked up," Barnabas said. Micah nodded his agreement.

"She won't be staying by herself. I'm spending the night," my father said.

I must have looked as shocked as I felt because my father bristled. He pulled me aside and quietly said, "Harriet, I know that when you set your mind on something, you follow through, damn the consequences. Until the security is completely set up, you're not staying alone. And since I'm sure you're staying...well, I'm staying with you."

"Dad, I don't have a guestroom." The apartment was tiny. It readily met my needs because I had no need of a guestroom.

"I've slept on a couch before, Harriet. As a matter of fact, I slept on the couch at our house for a solid week when you were starting school," he said.

"Really?" I had no memory of that.

"You cried the first day of kindergarten and I told you to stop making a spectacle of yourself. Your mother, rightly, pointed out that you weren't the only child having a difficult time with the first day of school. She hugged you and kissed you and assured you that you could do it...and then you did it."

"But why the couch?" I asked.

"Your mother said that I wasn't allowed back in our room until I learned what it was like to be kicked out of someplace where you were loved and pushed into an uncomfortable new experience. She felt my sleeping on the couch for a few nights illustrated her point perfectly."

My father, who rarely spoke of my mother, smiled. "She was right. I totally understood. That next week, I took you to school on my own and you simply said goodbye and walked into your classroom and I realized I'd missed a chance to be the father you deserved. So, tonight, I'm going to camp out on your couch and be that this time. I've got a bag in the car."

He turned back to the group and walked over to Miss Lonnie as I stood there stunned.

Kitty Meyers came over and patted me on the shoulder. "Honey, some people aren't very good at showing they care. I suspect your father fits into that category, but as a professional people-watcher, I can tell you that he does care in his own way. His way might not be your way, but with practice you can learn to identify it."

I watched my father mingle with my friends. He laughed a few more times at Lonnie. I didn't know what to make of it.

As my friends started leaving for home and my father walked Lonnie to her car on his way to get his overnight bag, I was left with Micah on the front porch.

"Thanks again for the doorbell," I said awkwardly.

"Your friend Barnabas said he'd help me hook up the security light and camera in the back tomorrow."

"I can't imagine that someone's coming back. I mean, how many dead bodies can someone have just lying about waiting to be disposed of?"

Micah shot me a look and I realized that some people did indeed have more than one body about. I gulped. It was easier to think that this was a one-off, but maybe the person who broke in made a habit of killing people.

"I'll be back with Barnabas tomorrow after work," Micah said firmly.

"You really don't have to."

Micah shrugged. "I'm hoping I get a good Yelp review from you."

I laughed. "If I don't go to jail for torching a body or worse, you definitely will."

We stood there for a few more moments, then he said, "Goodnight," in that low and slightly gravelly voice.

I didn't say anything, but I wondered if he could hear the sound of my heart racing. I gave a small wave as I hurried back inside.

Moments later, my father came in as well. "You really don't have to—" I started.

"Harriet, I really do. If I went home, I wouldn't be able to sleep because of worrying about you. At least on your sofa, I'll get some rest."

"You could have my bed," I offered.

"I—"

My father interrupted. "The couch is fine."

I gave in. "Okay. Let me go get some bedding and a pillow." I started toward the linen closet, but my father said, "Harriet?"

I turned. "Did you need something else?"

"Someone informed me in no uncertain terms that words matter," he said.

"Someone?"

"Lonnie. She said she's been volunteering for a woman whose mantra is *words matter* and she suspected no one ever told me that. And then she told me a daughter especially needs to hear the words. And I realized that your mother spoke for both of us and when she was gone, I never learned to do it for myself. So...Harriet I love you. This incident scared the life out of me. Hearing about your notes on the wall downstairs scared me even worse. Leave this to the police. Let's hope that it's over for you."

I felt a rush of emotion. He was right, he sucked at saying the words. But there were so many things he did that showed he cared. I sometimes didn't take the time to recognize them. But sleeping on my couch tonight would forever be a moment I'd remember...a moment that showed my father loved me.

"I love you, Dad."

Oh, I was still thankful I no longer worked at his office, but, as I thought about it, that had more to do with the work that I didn't feel was satisfying than with working alongside my father.

"Thanks for those words," I added.

Then I hurried down the hall to get him bedding.

Things were getting weirder and weirder.

Chapter Six

"As a potter there are only a few things I need. Clay. My wheel. And coffee…"
~Harry's Pottery: A Personal Journey

The next morning, I heard my father stirring. I got up and made coffee while he was in the shower.

When he came out, I said, "Help yourself. Do you want breakfast?"

"No, the new receptionist brings me a breakfast sandwich every morning. She said my diet was appalling and so she brings these egg white sandwiches with spinach and other things I choose not to ask about. Don't tell her, but they're growing on me."

That almost sounded like he was teasing. Which was a very abnormal thing for my father to do.

He went to my coffee-mug tree and stood in front of it for an abnormally long time.

That was a lot of abnormals for one morning.

"Something wrong?" I asked.

"Just trying to decide which one to try."

"You're welcome to any of them…they're all clean," I added.

"Your mugs have personalities. That one you made me for Christmas is my I-need-to-put-my-nose-to-the-grindstone mug. It's solid and hefty. That first one you made me after you started the studio, now that's one I use when I want to remind myself to be happy. I used it the morning I asked Phyllis out."

Whoa. Wait, what was that? "Phyllis?" I asked.

"The new receptionist."

"Oh." The breakfast sandwiches made sense now. "Where are you taking her?"

"How do you know she said yes?" he asked.

I snorted. "You're a catch. Of course, she said yes."

"We've already gone out a few times. She took me to that new Speakeasy downtown."

"Room 33?" I tried to picture my dad there and couldn't.

He nodded. "Back to mugs. That one you made me when you were in college and told me you wanted to pursue art...that one is the one I use almost every Sunday before we have brunch. It's the cup that reminds me to support your dreams and remember your life is your own."

I felt myself tear up. "Dad."

"Listen, I know we have difficulties and I know they're my fault. Phyllis tells me that I'm emotionally constipated." He shot me a wry smile.

I decided then and there that I very much wanted to meet this Phyllis.

"I just wanted to say that the thought of someone breaking in here while you slept...it is the scariest thought of my life. If something had happened..."

He didn't finish the sentence, but I got the gist.

And I realized that for years, I'd blamed him for my not pursuing ceramics from the get-go, and suddenly I realized how unfair that was.

If I'd been that sure of myself, I'd have gone after my degree no matter what he said. I think I needed to do something I wasn't passionate about to realize how much I wanted my work to be fulfilling.

Dad picked a mug and poured his coffee.

It was a hand-formed mug, rather than one of the wheel-thrown ones. That meant it was more rustic. I loved doing folk art pieces. I'd carved a huge maple leaf onto this one. I used WFA, an ecru glaze, in the inside, and Alberta Brown on the outside. I'd glazed the leaf in a warm orange. I'd fired it in the gas kiln which made all the glazes come out dark and warm.

"What does that one say to you?" I asked.

"It says, my daughter is a gifted artist and that even as time marches on, it's never too late."

"Too late for what?" I asked.

"To say I'm sorry I held you back. To say I'm sorry I'm emotionally constipated. And to say I love you again."

Part of me wanted to ask *who are you and what did you do with my father*? But I could see how vulnerable he'd made himself, so I said, "I wouldn't change anything about my journey to get where I am. I love my life. And I love you, too. Now, when do I get to meet this Phyllis? Sunday brunch?"

"Are you sure you won't mind someone else barging into our time?" he asked.

"Our time will still be our time...even if we share it with someone else." That sounded very zennish.

My father smiled. "Tomorrow it is. Well, as long as she's available. I don't like to presume."

Seriously, what had this Phyllis done to my father?

He finished his coffee and I said, "Wait a sec."

I washed out the mug and put it in a bag. "Take this one and remember I love you."

He hugged me, again something rare. We weren't a huggy sort of people. "I love you, too. And in case I haven't mentioned it lately, you are an amazing woman. Your mother would be so proud."

He left then. He had a mug in one hand and an overnight bag in the other.

Before he reached the door that led to the front staircase and then my front door, he said, "I'll keep checking in. Please, whatever you do, don't go poking around Junior's death. Leave it to the cops."

"I'll leave it to them," I said. Even as I said the words, I realized that I was lying.

It had been an odd exchange. The break in had scared my father. I wondered if this newfound openness— well, more open at least—would last.

I was still mulling over the change in my dad as I started my day at the computer, searching the county records. I found the names of the previous owners of the studio, Trisha and Tyler Tawny. I searched their names and found out Tyler was in jail and Trisha had disappeared from social media. No Facebook page. No Twitter. No Instagram.

I also Googled cremation—the optimum temperature range is between fourteen and eighteen hundred. I fired my Cone 6 pottery to more than two thousand degrees. If someone didn't know about the slow ramping of temperatures, it was easy to see how they'd think a body would have burned to ash overnight.

I put the information on my wall and went to work on my order. I left the closed sign in the window. Sunday and Mondays were my days off. I'd open Tuesday.

Then I got to work throwing off the hump.

I fell into the rhythm of the wheel.

Wheel throwing was very step oriented. I think it appealed to the same part of me that enjoyed contract work. Step by step.

You built a plate, pot, or cup the same way every time.

Oh, you could get a bit fancy when you finished it off, adding embellishments or finishing a foot. But the actual work of throwing remained the same.

I found the rhythm very soothing. Most of my thrown pieces were done by touch more than by sight. Maybe other potters work in different ways, but for me, not looking sometimes helped. That left me time to study my wall as I worked.

Tyler Tawny was the first suspect I could absolutely cross off my list. He was incarcerated, which in and of itself was a good alibi, but added to that, he might have lived here once, but that wouldn't explain how he'd know I had a kiln, where it was, or how to program it.

I couldn't rule out that he had some ceramic knowledge, but again there was the whole locked up thing.

So, I could state with pretty firm assuredness that Tyler Tawny wasn't the person who'd broken into my studio.

One down...everyone else to go.

Wait, I could cross me off the list.

Oh, the cops couldn't do that, but I knew it wasn't me.

Two. Two suspects off the list.

My father had a key, but I felt confident crossing him out. Maybe it was nepotism, but there was the added fact that he didn't have a clue on programming kilns.

Of course, whoever had programmed it hadn't had extensive knowledge or else they'd have known that the program they selected wouldn't have burned up all the evidence by morning.

Could my father be a suspect?

He had a key. He could Google how to work a kiln. But no matter how I twisted it, I couldn't imagine my father killing someone. Even more than that, I couldn't imagine he would leave the body in my kiln.

He loved me. Even at our most awkward moments, I knew that.

I remembered right after my mother died. I went shopping with him and for some perverse reason, I stole a bubblegum lip balm.

Looking back, I couldn't understand why I did it and I don't think even at the moment I knew why I did it. I had allowance money. I could have bought it. Or I could have tossed it in the cart and my father would have bought it.

But I simply slipped it in my pocket.

I got it out in the car, ready to put it to use when he asked where I got it.

When I confessed, he marched me right back into the store and made me return it. Then he paid for it.

Then I paid for it.

I'd been grounded for a month with a mile-long list of chores.

No, a man with that strong sense of right and wrong would never kill someone, then leave the body in his daughter's kiln.

When I finished a mug, I wiped my hands on my towel—I wore an apron and covered my thighs with towels when throwing because it is a very messy process—and got up to add a column to my wall. I named it, *People-Who-Didn't-Do-It*. I put me, my dad, and Tyler on the list.

There, that was an accomplishment.

I wedged another batch of clay and then started throwing more cups.

I worked my way through the rest of them, with thoughts of bodies in kilns, new hand-built mugs, and my father's atypical behavior this morning.

And maybe, in amongst all those thoughts that swirled along with the wheel, maybe there were a few thoughts for Micah McCain.

And maybe I was a bit happy at the thought of seeing him tonight.

And maybe it had been a long time since the thought of seeing a man again kept inserting itself into my thoughts this way.

And maybe I liked it.

***

At five fifteen, someone knocked on the back door. I opened it with butterflies in my stomach at the thought of seeing Micah.

It was Barnabas. I made sure I didn't let that quick spurt of disappointment show. I adored Barnabas. I saw that something wasn't right.

"What's wrong?" I asked as I pulled him into the studio.

"Long day. We lost one of our elderly dogs."

Barnabas took every loss hard. Even when he said it was for the best, it hurt him. I hugged him as I ushered him inside. I saw Micah walking toward us before I shut the door and held it for him.

"Thanks again, both of you, for setting up this camera," I said. "My dad's probably-aching back thanks you as well for saving it another night on my couch."

"Lady Bug, I would have felt better doing it last night." He turned to Micah. "Let's get started."

"We're going to need a ladder," Micah said.

"I know where it is. We're set," Barnabas said in a very melancholy way.

"He lost a patient today," I said to Micah.

"Ethel was a great old dog," Barnabas said. "She was a rescue and came from a troubled background, but she had a good life." He looked as if he were going to cry.

I patted his back.

"We can do this another day," I said. "Or I can help Micah."

He shook his head. "No. I know it's ridiculous to be this upset. I deal with this sort of thing every day. But Ethel was special. She hated me in the office. I mean, wanted to bite my face off every time she came in. We muzzled her, which only made her hate me more. But she lives close by and walks along the bayfront a lot. When she walked by, she always liked to stop at my place for a bone. She liked me a lot then."

"Barnabas is every dog in the neighborhood's favorite destination. He keeps a jar of bones on the porch, so even if he's not there, they can stop in for a snack," I told Micah.

"I get it," Micah said. "I had a dog growing up. Sandy. She was scruffy. I mean, she always looked as if she lived on the street. Even right after a bath, she was a mess. But she followed me everywhere. When she died I was fifteen. And at fifteen it's not cool to be distraught over a dog, so I skipped school for two days because I wasn't sure I wouldn't be able to not cry."

Barnabas led Micah out the back door and into the garage. Just before they walked through the door, I saw Micah pat my friend's shoulder and I discovered I liked Micah just a little bit more.

And that was weird.

I didn't know much about him other than he worked for my father, was serving as my lawyer, offered a room to someone he hardly knew, and comforted Barnabas.

Come to think of it, I'd dated and liked men who I knew less about.

I was tempted to stay at the back window in the studio kitchenette and watch the guys work, but I forced myself to get back to work. I had met my day's quota, so I allowed myself some fun.

I liked wheel throwing and that's what paid my bills—along with occasional legal work for my father—but my true ceramic love was hand building.

Time to make my father a mug.

I could throw one, but I wanted this one to come from the heart.

I pulled out a grapefruit-sized hunk of grey clay and wedged it into a spiral. My table for wedging—think of kneading bread, but rather than working air into flour and making glutton, I was trying to push air pockets out of the clay—was right in front of my chalkboard wall, which was now covered with Post-its and chalk notes.

How was I going to find out where my house's previous owner, Trisha, was?

I took a break and called Miss Betty. If anyone would know, it would be her. But she didn't have a clue.

I might be able to figure out something on my own, but... I thought of

Coco. Well, Colleen. She was a private investigator who occasionally did work for my father. I'd just spent my financial cushion on a new kiln, but I was sure she could find Trisha in a lot less time than I could.

Sometimes it was worth paying for expert help...even if I wasn't sure where I'd find the money.

I threw a piece of plastic over my wedged clay and called Coco and got her voicemail.

"Hi, Coco. It's Harry Lawe. Any chance you could find someone for me?" I gave her what little I knew. "And please, don't mention anything to my father."

I hung up.

Okay, that was a start.

Who else?

It had to be someone with at least a cursory knowledge of my studio...or *a* studio. They had to understand how a kiln worked, even if they didn't know how to program it properly.

That led me back to my *Wine and Mud* class. They should have been here last night, but my mom's group had understood when I canceled the class. They had at least a cursory knowledge of how a kiln worked.

We'd toured the entire studio, including the kiln room. I'd taught them all how the electric and gas kiln worked, and they'd all helped load my kiln a couple times. There's an art to it. The first firing—bisque firing—was the easiest for a novice to load. Pieces could touch. They could even be stacked together. This was a low heat firing.

The second firing was to Cone 6 most of the time in my studio. Two thousand, two hundred and thirty-two degrees. For that one, the pieces were glazed and couldn't touch because the process vitrified the clay and turned the glaze into glass. If they touched, they'd stick together. If the glaze got too close to the kiln shelf, it would stick there and that was a mess.

Firing to Cone 6 was a long process. The kiln was programmed to start at a low temperature (relatively speaking) and slowly ramp up to higher ones.

Whoever dumped the body in my kiln had used one of my preprogramed settings. It was a very slow rise in temperature.

Which is why there were still intact bones. If the firing had gone all the way through, those bones would have turned to ash.

I thought about my class as I pinched that ball of clay into a mug.

I took out my tool and smoothed out the ridges. I tapped the bottom to flatten it, then turned it over and tapped the rim until it sat fairly level.

I walked it over to the fan in the corner and turned it on low.

Turning it every five or so minutes to keep the clay drying at the same rate, in less than a half hour, I should be able to carve it.

I pulled out Post-its and, not wanting to use my student's names, I labeled them with initials.

B. Barbara Ann Miller. She was a tiny single mother of three. Her ex kept the kids every Friday night and Saturday, so our *Wine and Mud* class was her "me" time. She was young. Maybe mid-twenties. She'd married young and divorced young. She was maybe five foot two on a good heel day. I couldn't see her muscling a body into a kiln. I put a "*?*" on her note.

Not a body, I realized. Junior. He'd been on the school's basketball team and had been long and lanky. Even if he'd never gained another ounce, the sheer size of him would have made Barbara Ann getting his body into the kiln on her own next to impossible.

Unless she had help.

C. Charlotte Neiman was somewhere south of fifty. Or would it be north? I had no clue.

Her kids were grown and gone. It was just her and her husband. She was taller, and I knew she participated in CrossFit classes and triathlons. Of anyone in my class, Char was probably the most physically capable of tossing a grown man into a kiln. I put a star on her Post-It and wrote *athletic*.

I grabbed another one and wrote a *J.* on it. Julie Iron. I'd given her the key in the past when the class had come in to finish projects. She'd given it right back, but she could have had it copied. I put a star on her paper too, though I seriously had trouble thinking of any circumstance that Julie would hurt someone. She was a kind and gentle soul.

But I guess if you were a murderer, radiating that kind of sweetness was a good cover.

I underlined her star and wrote *opportunity*.

L. Liz Champion. She was the mother of teen twin boys and while she was a tall woman, maybe five seven, she was so thin that she looked as if a stiff wind might blow her away. From what I'd seen, her biggest muscle was her cheek muscles—she was always smiling.

I'd joked once that I'd never seen her frown. She'd laughed and said, "Sometimes I try to frown at the boys. It never takes and they don't buy it." She'd heaved a mock sigh and then burst out laughing.

I didn't want to put a star or even a question mark, but I was trying to be fair, so I went with the question mark and wrote, *too happy?*

Finally, there was *H.* Which if I'd been going alphabetically wouldn't be last. Helen Smith. She was solidly in the middle, age-wise and height-wise. She was an attorney. I'd met her through my father. He was a defense attorney. She was an ADA. Helen had come to the office more than once because of a case.

She'd also worked on high profile cases and she'd know about the legality and have seen what worked and didn't in covering up a murder.

She got a star and I wrote, *knowledge.*

I had my kids' class too but really, I had a hard time believing Lynn, Patti, Kathi, Britta, or Brenda had anything to do with Junior ending up in my kiln and frankly, I didn't teach kids how to use kilns. I didn't even bother putting them up on my wall.

I wasn't sure that brought me closer to any insights, but back when I was in school and working on a project, I simply started by collecting information. At some points all those facts would crystalize, and I would find a path to writing the paper.

I took my chalk pencil and wrote *Collect Info* at the top of the board.

My mug had dried sufficiently to start carving.

I decided to make a tree. The bottom was carved bark-like and the handle would be as well. The lip at the top was smooth, to make drinking and cleaning easier. But at the bottom, carved into the bark, I made a small heart. It wasn't something overly mushy, but I thought my father would understand it was my way of saying I loved him.

Barnabas and Micah came in the back door.

I put a bag over my mug so it wouldn't dry out any further. "How'd it go?"

"Even easier than the doorbell," Micah said.

Barnabas laughed. He seemed in better spirits than when he'd come in. "We could go into a business. How many attorneys and vets does it take to put up a light bulb?"

"Two," Micah answered. "One each."

They both burst out laughing.

"That was horrible," I said, trying to hide a smile.

"You're laughing," Micah said.

"I'm not. That was a grimace over you two and your equally matched lame humor," I said, though that was a lie. I had been smiling.

Barnabas took my phone and started to work his magic. Pretty soon he handed it back. "When someone is at either front door and rings your doorbell, it will ring through to your phone and you'll not only be able to see them but talk to them. And if they're out back, they'll trigger the motion detector and your phone will buzz. You can speak on that, too. Micah, go try out the back."

Micah walked out the front door, and pretty soon my phone buzzed and there he was in the back waving toward the camera that was tied into a flood light.

"Push this and you can speak." Barnabas pushed the button and said, "It works. Come on in."

Micah walked around toward the front door.

"I feel better knowing you can see what's going on out there," Barnabas said.

"I think I'll be fine. I suspect whoever brought Junior into my studio did it because of the kiln, not because of me. If I were going to dispose of a body, a kiln would be a good way to do it. If it had been in there longer and at a higher temperature, there would have been nothing but ash left. I Googled cremation," I confessed.

"Yeah, that's not going to look suspicious if the cops subpoena your computer," Micah said.

"This morning. I Googled it after I found the body. Well, after the attempted cremation in my kiln. If they search my browser history, there are no kiln cremation searches before poor Junior."

Micah still looked miffed.

"I just wanted to know. And now I want to know if you guys would like to get pizza. It's the least I can do since you set up my security."

"Sure," Barnabas said.

"Not necessary. Your father should be here soon with dinner."

"He was here last night and slept on my couch. Plus, I've got brunch with him tomorrow," I said.

"He's worried about you," Micah said.

As if on cue, someone rang the doorbell. I started for the door, but Micah said, "Try your phone."

I did and there was my father, a huge bag in his hand.

"Use the speaker," Micah said with the sort of glee that's mostly reserved for kids on a Christmas morning.

"Hi, Dad. I'll be right there, if Micah will let me stop testing the doorbell."

I heard my father's laughter over the speaker.

It sounded good.

Chapter Seven

*"Information. Every successful
potter builds off the past and
adds to the collected knowledge of the art."*
~Harry's Pottery: A Personal
Journey

I convinced my father that I was perfectly capable of spending my night alone in the fortress the guys had created. My father had been reluctant to leave, but I had to point out that the odds of me being struck by lightning were probably higher than the odds of me finding another dead body in my kiln.

I shooed all three men out of my house. I double-checked all the locks downstairs before heading upstairs for the night.

I'd just climbed in bed, ready to watch another episode of *Cereal Killers*, when my phone rang. It was Coco.

"Hey, that was quick," I said by way of greeting. "Did you find anything?"

"Got a pen and paper?" she asked.

I searched through the drawer in my end table and came up with both.

"Trisha divorced her husband after he went to prison and started using her maiden name again. Trisha Jenkins. She's got a small place at..." Coco spit out an address on Erie's east side, a phone number, then added, "She works as a bartender at *Down By the Bay*."

"Send me your bill, Coco. And thanks."

"Honey, this one's a freebie. I mean, after you discover a body in your kiln, you deserve a few breaks." She paused a moment and said, "You're not in any trouble, are you? I'm here if you need me."

"No. I'm back in the house and there's a new security system in place, so I'm back in business. It's all good."

"So why did you want to know about Trisha?" she pressed.

When you're evading an answer it's best to stick to the truth. "She used to own this house and I wanted to see if she had any keys left and/or knows who might have copies."

"Why not just change the locks?" Coco pressed. Her persistence was what made her good at her job.

"I did. I'm just compiling a list for the cops," I said, still technically the truth.

"I suspect that's not all. And I don't like what I think it might be. Give the detectives her name and let them ask her about keys."

I laughed. "I know how you feel. I don't like what's going on either. I didn't like finding that body in my kiln. I promise I'll talk to the detective. Thanks again, Coco."

I would absolutely talk to the detective...when I had some answers myself.

I could see the bay from my front window and I knew that *Down By the Bay* was only a short walk. I'd walked by it many times, though I'd never gone in.

I wasn't much of a bar person. If I wanted to hang out with friends, I wanted to be able to converse with them. Bars were too loud for that. And if I wanted to go out by myself...I just headed down to the studio.

But tonight, I decided I might need a drink. I threw some clothes back on, grabbed my keys, and headed out the door.

It was still early enough that I didn't worry about walking. And I could call an Uber to get home if I stayed too late...not that I planned to stay too late.

I was hermit enough that I hadn't given any thought to a bar on a Saturday night. It wasn't quite packed, but it was full.

I waited for a barstool to clear and studied the bartenders. One hipster looking guy wearing a plaid shirt and sporting a full beard and gauged ears.

The other was a willowy blonde with a full sleeve of tattoos. I thought she was young, like the guy who was bartending, but as I took a seat and she asked me what she could get for me, I realized she was quite a bit older than him. As in she could be his mother sort of older.

"Guinness?" I asked, because that was my go-to beer.

She nodded and a few minutes later, was back with a perfectly poured glass.

"Thanks. It's crazy down here tonight."

She nodded. "Yeah it is. It's not like this on weeknights, but weekends...?" she shrugged and headed farther down the bar.

She moved up and down the bar, getting drinks for patrons and for servers who came up with orders.

She was amicable, but not flirty or even overly chatty.

"Trisha," someone yelled.

Yes, this was the woman who used to own my house.

I was here.

She was here.

But I hadn't worked out what I wanted to say. What questions I wanted to ask.

As she approached me and my half-empty Guinness, I asked, "When you have a minute, could I get an order of fries? I'm from up the hill and found a dead body in my studio this week. I think I deserve a drink and to splurge on fries."

"You live up on Front Street?" she asked.

I nodded.

"The pottery store?" she continued.

There. She'd done the asking, not me, so it wouldn't seem suspicious to her. I sighed. "Yes. I'm sure you heard about it. It seems everyone in Erie has heard about it."

"Yes, I'm sure they did. Erie doesn't get many bodies in kilns. But I paid special attention because I used to own your house."

"You did?" I asked, hoping my acting skills were good enough that she thought I was surprised.

She nodded. "Then my louse of an ex lost it, along with just about everything else we had."

"I'm sorry," I said, genuinely meaning it.

She shrugged. "My therapist says to concentrate on what I can change. I can't change what happened, but I can change where I go from here on out. I've got a good job and a new place...someplace that's just mine."

"Hey, maybe you could help? The detectives were looking for people who had keys. Maybe you and your ex gave keys to friends?"

"Wait...you didn't change the locks?" She seemed as incredulous as everyone else who'd found out that I hadn't changed the locks.

I took a long sip of my beer. "No, I didn't. It's one of those mistakes that haunts me for a long time."

She smiled and nodded. "Hey, at least it was just not changing locks. For me, it was not changing men."

"Trisha," someone yelled.

"I'll be back." She hurried down the bar.

She seemed nice. But that didn't mean she couldn't have done it and put Junior into the kiln. At that moment, as if to reinforce my thought, she hefted a keg as if it weighed next to nothing.

Her ex was safely ensconced in prison, but could Trisha have killed Junior and tried to get rid of the evidence in my studio?

She'd have to have at least a rudimentary idea about kilns.

I wondered how much was online and if a novice could understand enough to start a kiln?

"Hang around for a bit. We'll talk more when things calm down a bit," Trisha said as she handed me a plate of fries.

I'd just popped a fry in my mouth when someone asked, "Is this seat taken?"

I turned to tell whoever it was that they could have the seat, but instead of a stranger I found..."Micah?"

"What's a nice girl like you doing in a place like this?" he asked as he took the seat next to me.

"What are you doing?" I countered.

"Sitting down and ordering a drink." He shot me a mega smile, hoping to blind me with its wattage into forgetting he'd followed me here. And let's be clear, I knew he'd followed me here.

"You know what I mean," I said sternly. "What are you doing at this bar at this time?"

"Can't a man go out on a Saturday night and take a seat next to a lovely lady?" He batted his eyelids beneath his glasses. And I realized just how blue his eyes were. I mean, if you could notice what color they were in a dim bar, they were pretty stand-outish.

I snorted my response. And tried to figure out how Micah had known I'd be here. I realized that I'd called Coco who worked with my father's firm. And Micah was part of my father's firm. Which meant...

"You talked to Coco?" I asked.

"About?" he countered innocently.

I glared at him.

He chuckled. "Maybe I did. And maybe she told me there was a great view at *Down By the Bay* and I should check it out."

He paused and added, "She didn't tell me why you were here or why she knew you were here. She was worried about you, that's all."

"Geesh," I muttered. "You find one dead body in your kiln and suddenly you're everyone's pet project."

"What's going on, Harriet?" Micah asked, all joking aside.

"Harry," I muttered and took another fry.

Micah reached out to help himself to one and I smacked his fingers away. "Order your own."

Now, I know that wasn't very kind. Micah had, after all, given me a room when I was all but homeless. Represented me when I was questioned by the police. And he'd put up a security system for me...and comforted Barnabas.

Still, he was annoying and intrusive. He seemed to think I couldn't handle myself.

And I could.

I realized how petulant that sounded, even in my head.

I nudged the plate at him and he helped himself to a fry.

"I'm worried about you," he said.

"You don't know me from Adam. Not really. You work for my father and because of him, you're acting as my attorney."

"Harriet—"

"Harry," I said through gritted teeth.

"Harry," he said patiently, which further set me teeth on edge.

I was feeling very toothy as he considered what he was going to say. That was an attorney move...take a second and think before saying something.

"Harry, I will admit we haven't known each other long, but I'm hoping we will know each other for a long time. So, every time we get together, we are simply laying the groundwork for a lifelong friendship by sharing details about ourselves."

Friends didn't follow friends.

"You're here checking up on me," I insisted.

"Maybe. Or maybe I'm just here because you're here and I want to know you better."

"Don't you have something better to do on a Saturday night?"

"No." He shot me a grin that had probably got him out of all kinds of trouble, but it wasn't going to work on me.

I was annoyed. I didn't need a babysitter, not even one with an endearing grin. "What else did Coco tell you?"

"Only that she knew you were coming down here and maybe I should come down as well. Why are you here?"

"See that bartender?" I nodded toward Trisha. "She used to own the house."

"What house?" Micah asked.

"My house. Her husband's incarcerated and she was forced to sell the house. I asked her who else had keys." I didn't add that she'd been as incredulous as everyone else that I hadn't changed the locks. But to be honest, her shock seemed so genuine that it made me believe that she really had no clue that any key she had might still work, which meant she hadn't dumped the body in my kiln.

"Why on earth didn't you just call Detective Dana?" Micah said sharply.

There. Now he seemed to be as annoyed as I felt.

I forced an anything-but genuine smile and asked, "Just what about our relationship makes you feel you can speak to me in that sort of tone?"

He had the good grace to look chagrined and said softly, "I'm worried."

That took the wind out of my sail. "I have to think after Trisha's ex-husband's run-ins with the law, she's more apt to talk to me than a cop."

"What if she was the one who put the body in your kiln?" he asked.

"I think she was genuinely surprised when she realized I hadn't changed the locks and even if she was the one who broke in, I suspect she's not going to try a repeat performance of stuffing me into the kiln in front of all these people."

He sighed.

Trisha came back. "What can I get you, Sugar?"

"A Glenlivet. Neat and a glass of water."

She brought him his whisky and he poured literally one drop of water into the glass.

"Really?" I asked.

"You're not a whisky drinker, are you? Just a bit of water changes the flavor. It sort of breaks things up and releases it."

He laughed. "That sounds technical, but in reality, it's how my grandfather and father drink their whisky."

I laughed.

And we sat at the bar, sharing fries and talking.

It was almost like a date, though it wasn't a date.

Micah seemed to feel as if he were my keeper.

A half hour later, Trisha came back and handed me a slip of paper. "I gave my key back to the bank. I have no idea what Tyler did with his. He's locked up for theft, so I know he didn't use it. And here are the other people who had copies and might still have them." She paused and asked, "How is everyone in the neighborhood? Is Miss Betty still next door?"

I nodded. "She's a fixture. She finally gave up driving."

"Thank god," Trisha said with a grin. "Her car had more dents in it than non-dents."

"She was a terror. But other than driving she shows no signs of slowing down. Barnabas is still down the street. He's trying to talk me into getting a dog."

"After what happened, maybe you should listen," she said kindly. "I don't know if that's any help, but I hope they figured out who broke into the house. Your house."

She added that last part as if to be sure I understood she made no claims on the house. I might have come here to see if she could have dumped Junior into my kiln. And I guess if I were a cop, she'd still be on my suspect list...but I wasn't, and I liked her. So, I said, "You should stop by and say hi to everyone."

She shrugged. "It's embarrassing. You marry someone and think you know who they are and then you discover they're someone else entirely."

"I think we all realize that we can't own someone else's mistakes. All we can do is our best to avoid too many of our own."

She laughed. "You are very wise. And maybe I will stop by. I'd like to see what you make."

"I'd like that," I assured her.

She got called away again and only then did I notice that Micah was glaring at me.

"What?" I asked.

"What on earth goes on in your head? You stopped here because there's a possibility she has a key and it seems as if someone picked your lock or had a key to get in. She could have been that someone and you invite her over."

"I don't think she did it. And her husband was a creep. If he were out, I'd think he might have done it. She shouldn't have to wear a scarlet letter on her chest because she married a creep. Sometimes people change."

I wasn't talking about Tyler. I was talking about Alex.

One day we were building a life together and I believed that we were happy. And the next...he was divorcing me.

"I hope she does stop in," I said defiantly to Micah.

"What just happened?" he asked.

"It's not you. It's me. I like you and want to be clear that spending time with you outside our lawyer-client relationship isn't about anything more than friendship."

"I think, despite your recklessness when it comes to murder, anyone you're a friend with can consider themselves lucky. But that doesn't really answer what just happened."

It was a statement not a question, but I knew he wanted an answer.

"When my ex decided to divorce me, he said he wanted to be happy. That's when I realized I wasn't happy and I deserved it as much as he did. So, I bought my place, spent a year renovating it and then quit my job and took up pottery professionally. That made me happy. I've built a life I love. I'm not looking for any..." I was going to say relationship.

I wasn't discounting a new relationship someday. But not yet. I wasn't ready to take a chance on a relationship yet, even if I felt a bit of a spark when I was with Micah.

I could ask about Millie, clarify who she was to him, but to do so might indicate interest. And I wasn't interested, so who she was to him didn't matter.

"...anything more than friendship. I just wanted to be clear."

He took a long sip of his whisky. "You are very clear. And like I said, being your friend would make me lucky, so I'll accept. And as a friend, I'll ask you not to invite potential murderers over to your house."

"It wasn't her," I said. "I know I can't prove it. But I'm not a cop and to be honest, I'm not even a working lawyer. I don't have to worry about pesky things like evidence. I know in my gut it wasn't her."

He sighed. "Drink your Guinness, Harry."

I pushed the fries toward him. "Help yourself to a few more before they go cold."

Friends.

Yeah, I liked that definition.

Micah had proven he was a good friend to have.

After we finished our drinks and fries, I paid our tab and left a generous tip for Trisha.

"I meant what I said," I told her. "Please stop in sometime."

She smiled. "I think I just might."

Micah and I walked along the bayfront sidewalk then back up the hill to Front Street without saying anything.

When we reached my place, his car was parked in the drive. "I'll wait until you're inside."

If we were something more than friends, this is where we'd kiss. But I'd set the boundaries and I knew they were for the best. I wasn't ready for anything more than friendship. And there was still the question of Millie. Current girlfriend? Ex? Not that it was any of my business.

Unless we kissed, then it would be.

But we weren't, so it wasn't.

"Goodnight, Micah."

"Goodnight, Harry."

I was getting ready to shut and deadbolt the door when he said, "Try not to get in any trouble tonight."

"I won't," I promised.

I locked the door and tried to sort out my feelings about Micah.

They were too muddled, and I was too tired to make any headway.

***

When I woke up the next morning, I was just as tired as when I'd gone to bed.

I realized I'd kept my promise to Micah. I hadn't gotten in any trouble, unless you counted my trouble sleeping. It felt like every time I shut my eyes, I fell into a dream.

Dreams of my ex.

Dreams of Junior.

And most disturbing of all, dreams of Micah.

Yeah, that's right. Dreaming about a body in a kiln made sense. I understood it. Dreaming about my ex leaving me...that happened from time to time.

But dreaming about Micah? Dreams that included a lot of kissing with a man who might not be on the market? Those were harder to understand.

I was a bit bleary-eyed when I drove to my father's home for our weekly Sunday brunch.

He lived on Erie's lower east side. And by lower east side, I mean he lived right on the lake. It was a modest home, but when you looked across the bay to Presque Isle, it was apparent that this was a million-dollar view.

A colleague once asked him why he still lived there. Dad looked at me and smiled. I didn't need him to explain it to me. I think that's one of the things that was so attractive about my house...I had a similar view. Mine wasn't quite as direct as his was, but it was there.

I knocked on his door.

I'm sure he wouldn't have minded if I let myself in, but once I moved out on my own, I started knocking.

Dad opened it and smiled broadly when he saw me. "Harriet, I hope you're hungry."

This was not his usual greeting or expression. I wasn't sure what was up, but I suspected something was. "I am starving. But I'm also in need of more coffee, if you have some."

My father shot me an *of-course* look and I laughed. That was more like it. Josiah Lawe always had coffee somewhere about. It wasn't always fresh and it wasn't always hot, but it was always strong and provided a nice jolt of caffeine.

"You look tired," he said.

"I didn't sleep well last night." I didn't mention having gone out to a bar and I certainly didn't mention Micah finding me there.

"I can imagine. I wish you would have let me spend another night. I know

137

you're a strong, independent woman, but everyone needs someone to lean on sometimes," my father said.

For one awkward moment I thought he might hug me.

That moment passed and our non-hugging won out, but for a moment, I hadn't been sure.

"Is she here?" a voice called from the kitchen.

My father didn't have a chance to answer because a middle-aged woman popped around the corner.

"There you are. You're Harriet of course, and I'm Phyllis," she said as she swept me into a hug. "I've heard so much about you. All your father ever does is talk about how amazing you are."

"I'm Harry to everyone but Dad," I said, still mid-hug.

"Of course, you are," she said as she let go of me. She took a step back, still smiling, as I studied her. Her hair had once been red and then probably threaded with grey. Now it was grey with faint patches of tired red. Her eyes were a brilliant blue and her smile was off the chart.

"I hope you like roast beef," Phyllis continued. "I asked your father, but he doesn't have a clue if you like it. He'd only say that he was sure you'd eaten it before. Come into the kitchen."

"Harriet would like some coffee," my father said.

"If it's not too much trouble," I added.

"Trouble?" Phyllis laughed. "Not even a bit of it. Although, if you're anticipating your father's coffee, you're out of luck. I think even calling it coffee is generous." She sniffed at him, but I could see the teasing in her eyes. And to my utter amazement, my father smiled back at her.

"I'd love to try yours," I said.

"Come on back," she said heading to the kitchen. I could no longer see her expression, but it wasn't hard to imagine as she laughed. "Here I am inviting you into your own kitchen. I'm horrible, I know it. I've sort of claimed the kitchen whenever I visit. It's just that what your father does in this kitchen is a crime."

"You're preaching to the choir," I assured her. "I grew up eating his attempts at cooking, don't forget. After all, I can't forget," I added truthfully.

I remember one of the first meals he cooked after my mother passed. Creamed tuna fish with canned peas on toasted white bread.

He'd tried so hard, so I'd eaten it that one time...but never again. Eventually we both learned to order take-out like pros.

"You poor thing," Phyllis said with a laugh. "Sit down and let me show you how it's done."

Within seconds I had a steaming cup of coffee in front of me. The smell was somewhere between ambrosia and heaven.

I took a sip and was pretty sure I could die happy.

And thinking that reminded me of the body in my kiln, so I took another long sip. "This is amazing."

"My father owned a diner for years. Good coffee was the cornerstone of our business," Phyllis said as she bustled around the kitchen. She looked very comfortable in it, as if she'd used it a lot.

"It really is amazing," I assured her.

"She hand-roasts her own beans," my father said. "Then grinds them."

I couldn't decide if it was pride or awe in his voice, but either one sounded good.

"Really?" I asked.

Phyllis blushed as she nodded. "It's nothing."

"And she bakes bread." My father shot her a look that was so filled with tenderness and...longing.

Yes, I was pretty sure I was right about the look he gave her. And that's when it sunk in, he and Phyllis weren't just friends. I realized that he loved this woman. I wasn't sure if he realized it yet, but it was there.

I watched the two of them banter as Phyllis cooked. There was a roast in a cast iron pan that to my knowledge wasn't my fathers. Mashed potatoes, green beans, and homemade rolls.

We dished up our plates in the kitchen and carried them into the dining room.

I was afraid that Phyllis was going to ask about the body in my kiln. I held my breath as I saw her wind up to ask something.

"So, tell me about your pottery," Phyllis said. "I've wanted to stop by and see your store, but I thought it was cheeky. I mean, either I'd just stop in and not introduce myself or I'd introduce myself and you'd think I was forward. It was quite the conundrum. So, I waited to meet you first."

I breathed a sigh of relief...pottery I could talk about. "Well, now that we've met, stopping in wouldn't be cheeky at all. I'd love to show you around," I said and realized how true that was.

"Tell me about what you do and what you like about it," she said. "I think giving up a safe career and trying something so different was very brave."

I shrugged. "I don't know about that."

I hadn't felt brave when I quit the firm and decided to take a chance on pottery. I felt as if it was something I had to do, but that didn't make it easy and it certainly didn't make me brave.

"I definitely think it was brave," she said staunchly. "Your father does as well. Right, Josiah?"

My father nodded. "I'll confess, I didn't understand it at first, but when I saw what you did, I started to understand. And when I realized how happy you were doing it, I was sure it was the right thing. And I also realize I owe you an apology."

"For what?" I asked, totally confused and wondering just what Phyllis had done to my father.

"When you came to me in college and told me what you wanted, I didn't listen. If I had..." He shrugged this time. "Who knows?"

My world was rocking, and I suspected Phyllis was the one standing on the boat, shifting things in unexpected directions.

But I was pretty sure it was a good rocking.

"Things worked out just the way they were supposed to. And if I hadn't gotten my law degree, I wouldn't be able to supplement my sometimes-spotty income and without that ability I'm not sure how I'd have made it through a few periods starting up the shop."

My dad said, "Still—"

And as he prepared to ramp up his apology, I realize I didn't need it.

I'd always held a bit of resentment that he hadn't listened to me when I came to him in college, but that feeling was gone.

Just acknowledging what happened was enough.

And I'd been truthful when I said that everything had worked out for the best.

"It's fine," I assured him. "Everything I've done has led me to this place I am right now. And it's a good place. Well, except for the small matter of a body in my kiln. Other than that, I'm in a very good place."

As we ate, I tried to reconcile my weird mushy feeling toward my dad. I'd always loved him, but there had been a distance between us. And though it wasn't totally bridged, I felt as if we'd come a bit closer.

I looked at Phyllis and felt as if part of the change belonged to her. Probably a big part of it.

I normally felt as if I had to steer our Sunday conversations, but that was BP. *Before-Phyllis.*

"So, tell me about your business," she said again.

And I did. I told her about the order I was pretty sure I was going to finish in time. I told her about my own work. "I love ceramic sculpture. I really don't sketch well. Two-dimensional art is hard for me. But sculpting? I love trying to capture something three-dimensionally. I think I like it so much more because 2-D is visual. 3-D is tactile. As soon as I finish this order, I have a new idea."

I could have babbled on forever, but instead I said, "What did you do before you went to work for Dad?"

I realized that when I quit, Dad went on a small hiring spree. He hired a new contract guy, Micah and Phyllis.

"I was a teacher. High school art. When I retired, I was bored within seconds, so I went to work for your dad for fun."

I cracked up. "Really? Working for my father is fun?"

That last part about working for my father for fun was funny enough, but the connection between what Phyllis had done and what I did deserved a bit of a laugh. I mean, my not-artsy-at-all father was now surrounded.

"So, my father has a daughter who owns a studio and is now dating a woman who taught art?"

"I like art," Dad said as both Phyllis and I continued to chuckle.

"Sure. You know the prints in Dad's office? When I asked what he wanted he said, 'Something blue'."

"Blue's a soothing color. Most of my clients can use some soothing," he said.

"I love the Erie theme you picked out," Phyllis said. James Sabol, Kevin-John Jobczynski. Local artists who captured bits of the city's history.

"I found another, older Erie artist the other day online. Don Lord. I found it at a studio in California." It was an oil painting for Erie's Perry Square. "I had to look him up, but he was indeed from around here. I was going to see if Dad wanted me to put in a bid."

"I do," Dad said.

"You don't want to check it out?" I asked him.

He shook his head. "I'll leave art to you and Phyllis."

It turned out Phyllis knew of Don Lord and assured me it was a good purchase. She finished up by saying, "Well, your father's office is lovely."

"Tell me about what you did in school," I said.

"I taught art history, drawing, and ceramics. I still volunteer at the Neighborhood Art House. I thought maybe, once we got to know each other, I'd ask you to come in and talk to the kids there. Maybe do a demonstration? But obviously, waiting isn't my strong suit. Ask your dad."

I looked at my father and I would have testified in court that there was the faintest blush in his cheeks.

"I thought he'd be a fuddy duddy about me working for him, so I said I'd sign something saying he hadn't used his position to make me date him," Phyllis said.

I hadn't known Phyllis long, but I couldn't imagine anyone coercing her, so I snorted.

She lowered her voice and said, "I wanted to ask him out immediately, but I showed some restraint by waiting a couple weeks."

Phyllis kept us both laughing as she launched into a stand-up worthy monologue about her students at the Art House. I occasionally glanced at my father and realized again that he was...besotted by this woman. Yes, that was the perfect word. He looked at her and I could see it.

And I was glad for it.

"...and Carrie knows everything about everyone, so I asked her..." Phyllis said.

And I realized we had a *Carrie* back in school. She was a bubbly cheerleader.

There was another girl who came to mind on the heels of Carrie. Lori. Lori knew everyone back in our school days and she knew everything about everyone now as well.

She was super active on social media. She posted on people's walls, started a group for our graduating class and posted pictures and anecdotes on a regular basis. When I'd started Harry's Pottery, she'd posted the link all over and I probably owed her for a least a dozen customers.

If anyone knew anything about Junior, it would be Lori.

Why hadn't I thought of her before?

The answer was obvious, because I was a potter not a detective.

But if I wanted to know what Junior had been up to since we graduated, Lori would be the person who would know. And if I could figure out what he'd been up to, maybe I could figure out why he was in my kiln.

And if I could figure out why he was in my kiln, maybe I could figure out who put him there.

"What are you thinking about?" Phyllis asked. "You had a faraway look in your eyes."

"I'm sorry. I didn't mean to be rude," I said.

She talked over me and said, "You weren't."

"You mentioned Carrie from your school and I thought about a girl in my class who knew everything about everyone. I see her on Facebook, but I haven't spoken to her in years."

"I'm glad I stirred up a nice memory," she said.

We went back to chatting through dessert. Phyllis made homemade pie. Pumpkin. Tons of real, made-from-scratch whipped cream.

"Phyllis, I haven't eaten anything this good since…" I shrugged. "I don't have a clue when, but seriously, this is amazing."

That was a lie. I'd eaten as well with Micah, but I felt odd mentioning him to my father, despite the fact that my father had been the one to set us up…well, at least as attorney and client.

Phyllis smiled, obviously pleased.

"Can I help with the dishes?" I asked as we got up to clear the table.

"No. I did most of them as I cooked, so I just need to toss the plates in the dishwasher. Why don't you and your father go visit for a while."

"We visited at brunch," my father said.

Phyllis *tsked* him, like some parent might tsk a child. "Your daughter found a body in a kiln. She's been through a trauma. Go talk to her and comfort her."

Then she shooed us from the dining room toward the living room.

Rather than look annoyed, my father grinned. "She's very bossy," he said.

"She is," I agreed, "but in a very nice way."

We stood in front of the couch. I was ready to sit as my father said, "Do you need comforting? We both know I won't be good at it, but I'll do my best."

I laughed as I sank onto the cushion. "No. I've got a security system and I think finding a body in your kiln is like being struck by lightning...it won't happen again."

My father nodded as he sat on the opposite side of the couch.

We both stared awkwardly at each other, then Dad launched himself down a legal conversation gambit.

I happily went along. I might not be a practicing attorney, but I could follow this conversation with ease. I sometimes wondered if my father wanted me to follow him into the law so that we'd have some common ground.

It had worked. No matter what was going on in our lives, we could always meet there, in the law. But today was different. I left my father's feeling better about...everything.

I had a lead to follow. Okay, so maybe Lori wouldn't pan out, but it was something.

I liked Phyllis.

And my father seemed happier than I'd seen him in a very long time.

It was a good brunch.

Chapter Eight

"Sometimes I binge-make a product.
I spent months making folk art Santas.
Then I moved on to other things.
But when a customer requested a
Santa I obliged.
And I easily fell back into the
rhythm of making them.
Revisiting the past, is in a way,
coming home."
~Harry's Pottery: A Personal
Journey

On Monday morning, I met Lori. She'd been very sweet when I direct messaged her on Facebook.

We met at *Ember and Forge*. It was a newish coffeehouse on State Street, just a few blocks from my place.

Exposed brick, lots of windows that looked out on Erie's main drag, State Street. Local artwork on the walls and tables and an old wooden sign they'd found in the basement of the building during a 1986 renovation...*Ship Chandlery* it announced.

I loved the bits of Erie history. The entire city reveled in our place in the country's history. The Brig Niagara and it's *Don't Give Up the Ship*. George

Washington's visit to Waterford. Misery Bay. Strong Vincent...

I got two large black house blends and chose a seat that looked out at the sidewalk while I waited for Lori.

She always knew everything about everyone and, to an introvert like me, that was an amazing talent.

I lived in my own little world and rarely knew anything about anyone.

What I so enjoyed about Lori back in the day was that she was never gossipy. She was full of sunshine. That's why she knew so much...people shared with her. And when she passed on their news, it was always with kindness. She bragged about friends' successes and commiserated over their pain.

I stared out the window. People walked by visiting. People walking dogs. Business people in suits and carrying briefcases or bags.

All those people just going about their lives.

Did they ever just stop and appreciate what they had?

My life had changed last Thursday morning. Just a few days ago.

I'd been mindlessly going about my business, not really reflecting on the fact that I was living my dream. But I had been.

Everything changed that moment I found a body in a kiln.

Not just anybody. Or *any body.*

Steve Summers, Jr.

What had he been up to since high school?

I was hoping Lori would know.

As if on cue, she was standing next to me. "Harry. I'd know you anywhere. Thanks for the coffee."

I grinned because I would have known her anywhere as well. She had dark hair, bright blue eyes, and a smile that truly radiated happiness.

"I'd know you, too," I assured her. "Thanks so much for meeting me."

She sat down in the chair across from me. "Anything for a fellow Bobcat."

I laughed as she brought up the school mascot. Then I grew uncomfortable. I didn't know how to ask what I needed to know.

I was officially the worst amateur detective ever.

WWQD?

What would Quincy do?

I didn't need to figure it out because Lori said, "So you want to know about Junior, right?"

"How did you—"

She interrupted me. "Harry, I might still live out in the county, but we get the paper and I even have that

153

newfangled thing, the Internet." She laughed then grew serious. "I'm sorry you went through that and I understand you want to find out who killed Junior and put him in the kiln at your place."

I sighed. "Yes."

"I don't know how much help I can be." She took a sip of coffee, then jumped in. "Junior tried college after school but quit before the end of the first term. He went to work for his father at *Summer Garage*. His father went to prison a few years ago, and Junior took over running the place. They could have lost it—his father has a ton of restitution to pay—but Junior and his mom each owned a third of it. The cops couldn't prove they'd done anything wrong, so they got to keep the business."

"What did his father do?" I asked.

"He ran a fencing ring but he never did business in the shop. He always met people in public places." She shrugged. "I didn't follow it that closely."

I obviously hadn't followed it at all.

"We've taken the car there a few times. Junior was exactly like he was in school."

Junior had been full of himself in school.

I generally steered clear of him...except that one dance at prom that someone had immortalized with a picture. The one the detective had showed me.

"We stopped taking the car to the shop because he was not very pleasant. Now, his dad had always been very friendly and amiable, but then he was a big crook, so I guess not everyone is what they appear to be."

"That's the truth," I said, thinking about my father and Phyllis yesterday. My father had appeared to be disappointed in me, but that wasn't the case. It had me reexamining things I thought I knew.

"They didn't mention a family in the paper," I said.

"His mom's been gone a long time. His dad's still in jail. Junior married Tanya Bryant right after he came back from college. They divorced a year later and didn't have any kids. I haven't heard of anyone else in the picture." She smiled. "But I don't know everything."

I snorted. "You know tons. I'm so out of the school loop that I don't even know where the loop is."

Then we chatted. Lori told me about her husband and the kids. She told me about the farm. "We're starting a CSA."

I must have looked as puzzled as I felt because she said, "Community Supported Agriculture. Basically, people sign up, pay a flat fee, and then get a share of our organic produce throughout the summer. If it goes well, we're hoping to expand and get some local restaurants involved. And..."

Before she got up to leave, I was taking a stack of the farm's CSA fliers to put out at the shop and had signed on for my own share. Local, fresh, organic vegetables with no work on my part? It was a no brainer.

"Thanks so much for meeting me, Lori," I said.

Her happy expression faded a bit and she said, "Listen, be careful. Don't go poking your nose into things that should best be left to the cops. You'll tell the detective to call me?"

I crossed my heart and said, "I will. And I'm being careful."

She snorted. "You have never been careful. You have always been brave and fearless."

"What would you call someone who gave up a thriving career to chase their dream? Brave," she answered her own question. "And fearless. But never dumb. Don't be dumb now. Leave the investigation to the cops."

"I will," I said again.

She gave me a look I'd seen friends' moms give them. One that said she wasn't buying what I was selling.

"I will," I said again. "And let's not wait until I have my next brush with the law to get together."

She laughed at that. "That sounds great. I'll be seeing you with your CSA produce next spring, but what about a get-together at your studio? I know a few of the girls from school who would love to come. And just so you don't think I'm gender biased, we'll ask the guys, too. Like I tell my husband, men do have a few uses."

I laughed. "That would be fun. And should I feel bad for your husband?"

"No. After all our years together, he still can't seem to get his dirty clothes in the hamper. Near the hamper. On top of the hamper. But in it? Too tough. So, feel bad for me, his poor wife." She laughed then, which made me think that she really didn't mind.

"As for the get-together. I'll put out some feelers and we'll figure out when. I'll talk to you soon."

We both left. She headed to her car and I walked back toward my place. I had another avenue to pursue. I could look into Junior's father's trial. Maybe there was something there.

For years I'd considered my law degree a waste of time. It had taken me away from my passion. But what I said to my father yesterday rang true. My ability to supplement my income by dabbling in the law was helpful. And now in this investigation, all my work in the legal system seemed useful. I knew how to get the records, I knew how to read the records, and with all the contract work I'd done, I knew how to look at data and collate it. There was a skill to looking at, analyzing, and finding relevance in information.

Maybe, there was something there in the records.

Speaking of something there, my phone beeped, telling me someone was ringing my doorbell. I turned on the app and there was Adi on the porch.

"I'm not home, but I'll be there in a sec," I said through the speaker.

"I'll be waiting," she said.

I turned off the app and walked at a faster pace. Adi was staring out at the bay as I walked down the block.

"Hey," I said.

"Hey," she replied. "I was going to go in and see if you needed anything, but you weren't here and my key doesn't work."

"Sorry. I changed the locks. And that new doorbell I put in works, I'm happy to say. Well, I didn't put it in. Barnabas and Micah did. With everything that happened, it seemed wise. I—" I started to say I'd get her a new key, but I realized I didn't want to. I didn't want anyone having access to my place. "There's a doorbell and camera system on my door, too. And floodlights and a camera in the back."

I figured putting out the word that the place was now monitored may dissuade anyone else from leaving a dead body in my kiln.

That was top on my list. No more kiln cooked bodies.

"That's smart," Adi said. She was tiny. Just barely over five foot, even though she said she was five five. She'd once said that no one would ever know her true height because no one would ever see her without heels. I looked down and indeed, her heels made my feet hurt.

Her four-year-old daughter, Nori, was already taller than I suspect Adi was without her boots. Okay, that was an exaggeration, but it wouldn't be long.

I unlocked the door. "Come on in."

"The police came to see me," she said.

"I'm sorry." I felt guilty, knowing my friends were being questioned.

"Don't. Answering their questions was a lot easier than finding a body in the kiln," she assured me.

I didn't want to talk about the body, so I asked, "Where's Nori?"

"Kev's got her today. Most of the time they stay at my house, but today he decided to take her to the zoo. She was thrilled. She always is when he spends time with her. I hate sitting around the house by myself and figured you could use some help. When are you reopening?"

"Tomorrow," I said. "I can't afford to keep the business closed any longer."

"Then let's get to work cleaning this place up," she said with a chipper smile.

And suddenly that sounded like a great idea. I really didn't want to be alone. "Thanks."

We cleaned like it was our job. Adi said as much and we cracked ourselves up.

The police really had been respectful as they searched my place. Adi tidied up the front and I went to work in the back.

I'd just about finished when the delivery guy brought the new kiln.

My old one was great, but this one was even better, not even counting the part about it never having had a body in it.

The delivery guy helped me hook it up and level it, and I thanked him profusely. When he left, I started fussing with it.

Each kiln has a personality. I could run the same program in two kilns and get different results. I could run the same program in the same kiln with the same glazes and get different results. Thankfully, this order was for bisque-ware. It's the state you fire ceramics to before you glaze it. It's harder than greenware—dried raw clay—but it's porous enough that the glaze fuses to the ceramics as you fire. The glaze becomes glass at that point.

I was anxious to try out the kiln. I had just finished my fussing, when I heard the bell on the front door buzz. I didn't bother pulling out my phone to check who it was. That seemed lazy. Instead, I headed out to the showroom and saw Adi, Nori, and Adi's ex, Kev.

I'll confess, I didn't like the man. I was pretty sure he hadn't treated Adi well when they were married and I'd seen for myself how he treated her now that they were divorced. It wasn't always pretty.

"...you said after dinner," Adi was saying.

"Nori needs a nap and wouldn't take one for me."

"Aunt Harry," Nori called, running to see me.

"I'm going to take her back with me," I said, giving Adi and Kev space to finish their argument in private.

I took her into the studio and shut the door so she wouldn't have to hear her parents fighting.

"Would you like some clay?" I asked.

"Is it dead clay?" she asked. "Daddy said you got dead ones. He says your killin' 'em. I don't want no dead clay."

I suspected Kev had said something about Junior and felt anger. No child should hear something like that. I might not have a kid, but I was pretty sure I wouldn't even play the news these days with one in the room.

"Your daddy was just being silly," I said trying to make light of what she'd heard. "I don't have dead clay. Clay is made of rock and sand. Not people."

"Oh. Yeah then. I want to try to make a bird. Mommy put a bird feeder out back and we got some cards coming," Nori said, accepting my explanation without question.

As I got her an apron and a hunk of clay, I tried to decide what she was talking about. It took me a second. Then I hit on it. "Cardinals?"

"Yeah, they're red. Well, the boy's red. The girl's sort of brown, but she's got this red kind of beak and they're always together. Mommy says they stay together forever," she said with a very un-childlike sigh.

"I don't think I knew that," I said.

"Yeah. My daddy didn't know it. He left and made Mommy cry. If he was a cardinal, he wouldn't of done that," she said with all the surety of a four-year-old.

"Sometimes moms and dads don't stay together, but they always love their kids," I assured her.

Even when my father and I didn't see eye-to-eye, I always knew he loved me.

Nori dropped her voice to a whisper. "Daddy thinks I'm a pain in the...butt." She said the word *butt* with the proper amount of childhood mirth. "Sometimes when I want to go home, I just whine a lot and he takes me."

Like today, I realized.

Mystery solved. That's why she was home so early.

Not wanting to delve any further into her relationship with her father, I started to shape the clay in my hand. My professor had used this particular clay when I was in school and it was still my clay of choice for hand-building projects.

I made a simple ball shape and pinched out some wings and beak. I didn't say anything to Nori, but I caught her watching and imitating my actions.

I really tried to avoid teaching people how to go about their clay-ing. There are specific techniques that don't work well and some that work better, but most of the time, with a little know-how, students could accomplish their goal for a project. If they asked, I was happy to share tips or suggestions, but mainly I let them do their own thing.

I found this particularly helpful with kids.

I'd seen Nori, or the older kids in my class, build projects I was sure wouldn't work...and more often than not they surprised me and did work just fine.

So, Nori and I sat and built birds while Adi and Kev continued their discussion in the storefront. I was thankful that the glass was thick enough to block most of the conversation, though I could see from their expressions it wasn't going well.

"Ta da," Nori said, holding up a fair facsimile of a bird. "Can you fire it now?"

"It has to dry, remember," I told her. "But we'll set it in the kiln room. It's warm in there and it will dry faster. I'll fire it when it's dry."

"Thank you, Aunt Harry," she said with manners that would make Adi proud. "Can we—"

Kev stormed through the door, interrupting whatever she was going to ask. He came up to Nori. "I came to say goodbye, kid."

She held her bird aloft. "I made a cardinal."

"Nice," he said without looking. He kissed her cheek and paused a long moment. He said my name, just, "Harry."

I thought he was going to say something more to me, but he just shot me a scowl and stormed back out of the studio, slamming the door. I watched through the window as he said something to Adi, then left.

Nori sighed again in a totally too adult way. "So, you can't cook it today?" she asked again.

"No. Remember, we have to let it dry to..."

"Leather-hard," she said, using the correct term.

I nodded. "Right. But hopefully next time you visit, it will be ready for you to glaze. I have a great red glaze that will work for your cardinal."

"Can I make his wife?" she asked.

"Absolutely."

I went and got another chunk of clay for her. I was just sealing up the rest of the bucket when Adi came back.

"Are you bothering Aunt Harry?" Adi asked her daughter.

"No. Me and Aunt Harry are building birds. She's gonna let me glaze them next visit. I'm making our cards."

"Cardinals," I said.

"Yep," she agreed.

Adi looked at me and I saw she was asking if Nori was being a pain and I gave a small shake of my head. I adored Adi's daughter.

When Adi worked, Nori came along more often than not. She knew a lot about ceramics for a four-year-old and was always so much fun to work with.

"You finish Mrs. Cardinal. I wanted to show your mom what needs done out front," I said.

"Okay," Nori said.

"And remember..."

"Don't touch nothin' else 'cause some of it might not be good for a little girl," she said, parroting back what I'd said to her frequently. I reiterated this rule over and over again with my kids' class as well. I was careful to move sharper tools up when they came, but there was always a chance they could get into something.

'Mommy says I got to respect other people's stuff," Nori continued. "And I promise I won't. I remember."

"I'll be right back," I said.

Adi and I went into the showroom and I shut the door. The glass between my working studio and the showroom meant we could see Nori.

"Is everything okay?" I asked.

Adi might work for me, but first and foremost, she was a friend.

"Kev was being difficult. Nothing new there."

I wished I could say something to make it better. "I'm sorry."

"I think he's using again. I told him not to come get Nori again until he was clean, but..." She shook her head. "It's hard to see him like this. He had so much promise when he was younger, but now? There's nothing I can do to save him. I told him if he came by to see Nori while he was using, I was going to turn him in. I think he would have hit me if you hadn't been looking in. I've never seen him that angry before."

"Do you want to stay here for the night?" I asked.

She smiled. "You're a good friend. We'll be fine. I thought after he got busted a couple years ago he was scared straight, but it doesn't look like it is going to stick."

Kev had been busted for dealing. I never heard how he'd gotten out of jail time and, while we were friends, I'd never felt comfortable asking Adi. She told me once that when she looked at her ex she could see the man he ought to have been and it broke her heart.

I walked a fine line, trying to support her as much as she'd allow without dredging up old memories that hurt. I tried to listen when she wanted to talk and just be there when she didn't.

"He wasn't like this when I married him," Adi said softly.

I wasn't sure if she was telling me that or reminding herself. "I know."

"It's funny how you think you know someone and it turns out that you don't even have a clue. If it were just me, I wouldn't care. I'd close the door on that chapter of my life and just move on. But there's Nori. I know no matter what, Kev and I will always be connected through her and I try to do what's best for her."

I nodded as the front door of my closed shop opened. I was about to say *we're closed*, when I saw who it was.

"I saw your ex leave. Is there a problem?" Barnabas asked.

And that's when I realized I might as well be invisible.

Barnabas only had eyes for Adi.

I was not a matchmaker by trade or temperament, but it would have been impossible to miss the fact that my neighbor liked Adi.

As I thought back, I realized that more often than not, if her car was at my place, so was Barnabas. I worked hard to hide a smile. The very immature little girl in me wanted to sing, *Barnabas and Adi sitting in a tree*, but I somehow managed to contain myself.

And I suddenly suspected she was no longer noticing me any more than Barnabas was. I was a third wheel.

"If you ever have a problem with him, you just have to call..." It wasn't a complete statement. It just hung there. Barnabas didn't add Adi could call him, but it was there hiding at the end of the sentence. What he was saying was, *you just have to call and I'll drop everything and come running.*

Watching the two of them, I realized how perfect they could be together. Barnabas was a big man, and I think most people saw that. Just that. But when you got to know him, you realized that being a big man just meant he had more room for a soft, gooey center.

"Barnabas," Nori hollered as she burst through the door and launched herself at him.

He caught her, clay and all, and listened and she chattered away about her newest projects.

As he followed Nori into the studio, I watched Adi as she watched him go. And I knew that in addition to figuring out who put Junior in my kiln, I wanted to find a way to give my two friends a chance at the happily-ever-after they both deserved.

The happily-ever-after I suspected they could find with each other.

Chapter Nine

"So much about pottery is happy happenstance. It's allowing yourself to experiment and not worry about what happens next. It's a skill that works in life as well as the pottery studio."
~Harry's Pottery: A Personal Journey

I turned the sign on the front door from *Closed* to *Open* the next morning.

It had been less than a week.

Less than a week since I'd found a body in my kiln.

Not just any body...an old classmate.

So much had happened since then. It felt more like weeks. Or a month.

Still, I was determined to get my life back on track.

I had a quota of mugs to finish today.

Then I was going to find those court documents on Junior's father.

I took my last sip of coffee, then started wedging clay. Some ceramic artists aren't fans of wedging, but I found a comfort in the rhythm of it.

I wedged multiple balls of clay, then bagged them. That way I could sit at my wheel and not get up.

I exchanged wedging-rhythm for wheel-rhythm.

Slam the clay as close to center on a batt.

Seal the edge of the clay to the batt to stop it from slipping

Wet my hands and the clay.

Pull the clay up, push it down to truly center it.

Repeat until it's dead center.

Wet my hands again.

Open a hole in the clay.

Form a mug.

Cut that mug off the giant lump of clay.

Wet my hands.

Make another.

My thoughts were free to travel at will. I thought about nothing in particular. I thought about everything.

This. This is what I'd missed for days.

Working at the wheel was meditation. Maybe almost like a prayer. I felt connected and yet removed. I felt a part of everything, and yet removed from it as well.

I was enjoying the moment when the bell rang, indicating I had customers. I waved through the window, then finished the last mug. I cut it from the batt, then wiped my hands on my apron and went through the door into the storefront.

"Hi. Welcome to Harry's Pottery," I said to the three middle aged women who'd come in.

"Are you looking for something specific or just browsing?" I said in my best merchant voice.

The tallest of the three said, "We read about you in the paper and thought we'd stop in and check out your shop. We didn't know you were here."

"We love to shop local," said the shortest of the three.

I didn't comment on reading about me in the paper. The Erie Times had done a lovely piece on me when the store opened, but I suspected that wasn't the article they were referring to. I forced a smile and said, "Please feel free to look around. Let me know if you have any questions."

"Are you the owner who found the body?" the middle-sized brunette asked.

I'm not in the habit of lying, but I didn't owe these women an answer. They were chasing the macabre. So rather than answer, I hedged.

"I just work here," I said. It wasn't exactly the truth. It wasn't exactly a lie.

"Oh," the woman said, looking disappointed.

"What were you looking for today? Harry's Pottery has a complete dish set, there are lots of mugs, and some sculptural forms."

"We'll just browse," said the tall one, obviously the talker for the group.

I watched as they made their way around the room, picking up various pieces and examining. Hefting a mug here and a mug there.

Ceramics should be beautiful to look at, but more than that, they should have the proper *feel*. For a moment I thought that this woman was doing that, testing the feel of the piece before she bought something. I loved watching people interact with my pottery. I loved seeing what attracted them.

As I busied myself at the counter, I tried to watch serendipitously. On the far side of the shop, they stopped and chatted quietly.

They reminded me of the sparrows that sometimes swarmed my birdfeeder. Or Nora's cardinals.

Chirp, chirp, chirp.

Then, as one, they walked back to me.

"Did you find something?" I asked.

"We were wondering if we could see *the* kiln," the tall one asked. She put emphasis on the word the, letting me know exactly what she was asking.

"Pardon?" My surprise was genuine. No one had ever asked to see the kiln room before, but then I guess I'd never had a kiln that had cremated a body before.

"We'd like to see where they found the body," the short one said, just to be sure I understood.

"I'm sorry. The studio is off limit to shoppers. The owner is very firm about her creative space," I said.

Again, they all had that look of disappointment.

"Can you tell me which pieces out here came out of the kiln they found the dead body in?" Tall asked.

"All of them," I said, realizing myself that everything in my showroom had been in the dead body kiln. Granted they'd been in there pre-dead body, but still. I felt myself shudder as the macabre crew twittered their way through the shop and selected their pieces.

I rang them out with a professional smile on my face. I thanked them for shopping and tried to remind myself that it was a big sale and the shop needed that.

As they left, the tall one said, "You should tell the owner she could make some stuff in that kiln and sell it at Halloween. She'd make a mint."

I smiled and said *thank you.* As soon as the door shut, a cootie attack hit me. It was worse than last month when a thousand-legger in the basement crawled over my foot.

Thankfully, I'd been wearing shoes.

But that didn't stop the cootie attack.

I'd almost finished when the door opened and another group of customers came in. "Is this where they found the body in a kiln?" a woman asked before I could say, *Welcome to Harry's Pottery*.

I nodded and said, "Please let me know if you need any help with the merchandise," then picked up the phone and called Adi. "Want to pick up some hours   today?"

***

I'll admit that as soon as Adi came, I hid in the studio.

Now, working in plain sight, with only a huge window standing between me and the shoppers might not seem like hiding, but that window was a great barrier. I concentrated on throwing, not on people.

I didn't come out front again until Adi shut the door and switched the sign to *Closed*. I rinsed off my hands and walked out front.

"Thanks," I said. "That was crazy."

Adi nodded. "I think this qualifies as a record-breaking sales day."

"I don't know if I can be proud of that. Those shoppers came to see where the cops found the body. It was really quite macabre. They didn't come because of my work."

Maybe that was the part that stung the most. Maybe I wanted customers to see what I did as art, not as some curiosity that had to do with finding a body in my kiln.

"Maybe," Adi said slowly, "but they bought things because your pieces are beautiful. I sold your big *Dryad Emerging* piece to one woman. She's bringing her husband with her to pick it up tomorrow. She was nervous about moving it on her own. I promised I'd pack it up tonight, so it was ready for them tomorrow."

"You sold it?" I asked.

The production pieces I was making now were my bread and butter. But pieces like my Dryad were my passion. This one took me months of carving a two-foot tree with a woman emerging from it. It was probably the most delicate piece I'd ever made. I put an absurd price on it because frankly, I wasn't sure I wanted to sell it. It was, in a way, a physical representation of what I'd done. I'd left one thing to become another.

I'd left a marriage and found myself.

I'd left the law to become a potter.

And as much as I referred to what I do as a craft, maybe on occasion what I do is art. If so, Dryad was art.

"She really paid that much for it?" I asked weakly.

"She did. Without batting an eye. And just so you know, she wasn't one of the macabre masses. She didn't even ask about the kiln or the body."

"Wow." I'll admit, I was glad my Dryad wasn't going home with a dead-body kiln chaser.

Suddenly, my worries about money were abated for the moment. Those funds would keep the lights on for a while.

"Wow," I said again.

"You're happy?" Adi asked, grinning.

"I am. I never thought it would sell." I walked over to the piece. "I think I'll miss it."

"You can make something else like that."

I realized she was right. "I can."

I finally asked, "Was it as bad as it looked like through the window?"

"No, it wasn't bad at all. People were curious. And that's why they came in, but once they were here, they bought because your work is beautiful."

"Thanks. I don't think I can face their curiosity though. Do you have any interest in picking up more hours this week? I'd be grateful for whatever you can do."

"Yes. Nori has preschool on Thursday. I'll see if Mom wants to keep her non-school hours then like she did today. I'll text you tonight after I see what I can come up with."

"I know you have stuff to do for work," I said, offering her a way out. I didn't want her to feel sorry for me.

"The beautiful thing about programming is, I can do it when Nori's in school, or after she's in bed. It gives me flexibility. It means I have time to help out a friend when I need to."

I tried not to let my relief show, but I was pretty sure I didn't mask it very well as I breathed a huge sigh of relief. "Great. Thank you."

I took a bunch of pictures of *Dryad Emerging* before we packed up the piece in an oversized box with plenty of bubble wrap.

"It sold," I said as I ran a finger over her.

"It did. You are a gifted artist," Adi said. "You have a unique way of looking at the world that's mirrored in your pieces.

Even the simplest mug has a sense of that view and artistry about it."

Having people refer to what I do as art made me uncomfortable. I felt as if I were putting on airs. Craft seemed like a less presumptuous term.

Maybe if I'd stuck with ceramics in school I wouldn't feel like such an imposter but most days that's just how I felt. Like an attorney who was posing as a potter.

Right after I opened Harry's Pottery, my old professor, Professor Bert, stopped in for a tour. I said as much to him and he told me that in some cultures craft is considered the highest form of art. That sort of blew a hole in my comfortable term.

"Thanks," I simply said to Adi. "I'll see you tomorrow if you can."

"I'll see what I can pull together for you," she promised. "I'll text a schedule."

She left and I closed up the storefront, locking everything, then double checking all the locks. I went up the back stairs and poured myself a beer before I fired up the computer.

Then I got down to work on my new side gig...who killed Junior.

Pennsylvania has a great website for court cases. Some of the information about cases was right there and forms for requesting the rest were readily available.

I started printing, downloading and filling out forms.

Then I went to the Erie Times News website and started searches on articles about the trial. I did web-searches on it, and on Junior and his father.

I didn't stop to read anything, I simply located and printed.

I know I could have read the pieces on my computer, but as a holdover from college, I very much preferred paper in hand and a pack of highlighters.

I'd just started a web-search on the Junior's garage itself when my phone buzzed.

Someone was at the door.

I opened up the app and breathed a sigh of relief when I saw Micah standing in front of the camera.

"Hold on a minute," I said through the speaker.

I went down the front stairs and opened the door to my apartment, on the other side of the porch from where he was standing.

"What brings you out?" I asked.

He held a takeout bag aloft as he walked across the apartment side of the porch. "I know you reopened today. I thought I'd bring dinner. And if you already ate, I'll eat mine and you can save yours for lunch tomorrow."

"I haven't eaten," I said. As if to verify that fact, my stomach growled.

"Great," he said. "Are you going to invite me up?"

I knew I was going to, but I felt as if I needed to assure him that I was capable of taking care of myself. "You don't have to keep checking on me," I said with a smile, to keep my words from being too harsh. "I was in a cop-free zone today."

"The cops aren't why I'm here," he said slowly. "The dead body isn't either. I came to see you. I was afraid you'd say no if I called first, so I opted to follow the old adage, that it's better to do it and then apologize after if necessary. Is an apology necessary?"

He shot me a look that I was sure was supposed to be contrite, but he didn't manage it very well.

I laughed as I opened the door and let him in. "No, it's not."

He came up the front stairs, through the dark living room and into the dining room. "Whoa."

I looked at the table and laughed. "This is how I work. My father always used to complain my office looked like a hurricane swept through it, but the piles made sense to me."

The printer was still chugging away.

"What are you researching?" he asked, still eyeing the piles of paper.

"Come into the kitchen, we'll eat there, and I'll tell you."

As I ate Pad Thai sitting next to Micah at the counter, I told him about Junior, his dad, and the shop. "His father's incarcerated, but that doesn't mean this doesn't have something to do with him. I'm going to do some reading and see if I can find a connection."

"Did you call Detective Dana?" he asked.

"I really don't have anything to tell her yet. I thought I'd wait until I go through all this. There might not be anything here. This might not be connected to Junior's dad."

"But it's a lead," he insisted.

"One that any good detective probably is already chasing down," I pointed out.

"If you believe that, then why are you chasing it down too?" he countered.

I slurped a noodle then answered honestly. "Because I don't know if she is a good detective. And if she's not, if she's not looking at this kind of thing, then I could be in jeopardy. I knew him. He was found in my kiln. On the face of things, it would be easy to just assume I was the primary suspect and focus on me. But if they're only focusing on me, they might miss out on other leads."

"You're forgetting about motive," Micah pointed out. "You don't have one, do you?"

I shook my head. "No, I don't have one, but if Dana's not a good detective, then who knows what she'd think."

"You'll call her tomorrow?" Micah pressed.

I wanted to say no. And if I did say yes, I wanted to cross my fingers behind my back while I did it. But he looked so earnest I sighed and said, "Yes. I'll call her tomorrow."

"Great. Let's dig in after we finish eating."

"What do you mean?" I asked. Not sure if he'd brought dessert and I missed it.

"Two eagle-eyed lawyers are obviously better than one. Let's go dig through what you've found and see if we can find a connection between Summer's father and his murder."

Ah, no dessert just data.

We finished our meals, then went out to the living room. We ended up on opposite sides of the couch. Micah took off his jacket and tie and kicked his feet up on the coffee table after he saw me kick up mine. I looked up from a very verbose description of Junior's garage and realized that Micah was wearing socks with small turkeys all over them.

I laughed and he looked up. "Something funny?"

"Not in what I'm reading. Seriously, using ten-dollar words doesn't make you sound any smarter. Someone wrote this report with a thesaurus in hand. No, I was admiring your socks."

He held his left foot up and said, "Mom sends me weird socks all the time."

"Why?" I asked.

"When I was little, we had a dog who ate socks. He got them out of the laundry basket, out of the basement laundry room and maybe sometimes from under my bed. I frequently ended up wearing socks that didn't match. And when I was studying for the bar, I jokingly told my mom I wasn't worried about buying new suits if I passed. I was worried about making sure I always had socks that matched. It was just a joke, but when I passed, she handed me a box she'd been saving. It was filled with socks. Although no professional looking black socks. Ones like this. I have socks for every holiday you can imagine. I have them for... Well, let's just say, I'm always prepared. And I always have a matched pair of socks."

It was endearing. I pictured his mother, tiny, round with a dimpled smile packing up boxes of socks for him. She sounded marvelous.

I wondered if my mom would have been that kind of mom? I hoped she would have.

It probably felt nice.

I stared at Micah, sitting so casually and comfortably on my well-used couch and realized I'd only known him since Thursday. I'd met him and Dad's other new attorney before at the office, but it had been just a passing this-is-my-daughter, this-is-the-one-of-the-attorneys-I-hired-since-you-left sort of introduction.

I wouldn't count that as our first meeting. I'd count Thursday as the day we'd truly met.

He looked totally at home on my ratty couch, pouring over documents with me.

"Penny for your thoughts," he said.

I realized I'd been staring, and he was staring back at me.

"No attorney worth their salt gives up their thoughts for just a penny," I said primly, stalling for time.

He just waited.

I sighed. "I was thinking that it feels as if I've known you a lot longer than a week."

"Is that a good thing or a bad thing?" he asked.

"Time will tell. Did you find anything?" I asked, ready to change the subject.

He accepted my answer and said, "Not much. Senior pleaded guilty, but at first tried to qualify his plea. The judge wouldn't accept guilty with qualifications, so he finally just pleaded guilty."

"Wait, that ties into a report I found." I dug through one of my highlighted pages. "Here. It was in the paper. The reporter overheard Senior say, *'I know who rolled. He'll get his. Everyone who's part of this witch hunt will get theirs.'*"

Micah shook his head. "I can't imagine his own son turned on him. And more than that, I can't imagine a father arranging to have his son killed then burned in a kiln. Even a really bad father."

I sighed. "I know. It doesn't make sense. It doesn't make sense...yet. But it's a piece of the puzzle. When we get enough pieces, we might be able to see the bigger picture."

I set both pages aside...the one with the quote, and the one where Senior pleaded guilty.

I'd add it to my board tomorrow.

I realized that though the board wasn't visible from the shop, it would be visible to my *Wine and Mud* class, and to the kids' class as well.

I could move it upstairs, but to be honest, the apartment was so small I didn't have room to spread the information out. I needed some way to cover it up when people were in the shop.

I was mulling over how to cover my Idea Wall, when Micah cleared his throat. "You still there?"

I gave myself a little shake. "Sorry, I was thinking."

"Did you make any headway?" he asked, nodding at the papers.

I shook my head. "No. But I'll keep digging."

"And you'll call Detective Dana," he said with insistence.

I nodded. "Yes."

"And you'll do your digging via the Internet, not by going to chat with suspects in person."

"It was a bar," I said. "A very public bar."

He snorted. "Being your attorney is going to be a fulltime job, isn't it?"

Before I could protest that I didn't need a keeper, he was leaning toward me as if he were going to kiss me.

"Millie," I blurted out, stopping that kiss in its tracks.

"What?" he looked truly puzzled.

I was many things, but I wasn't a cheat...and I wasn't someone who let herself kiss a cheat. "Who is Millie? You let me use her bath bomb, but you never said—"

"My sister."

"Oh." Phew. Not a cheat.

And yet, if he had a girlfriend, I'd have a legit reason not to kiss him. I never intended to not date again, but I'd been busy starting a business, so it hadn't been a good time. Finding a body in a kiln...that couldn't be a good time either.

And yet...

"I wouldn't kiss you if there were another woman in my life," Micah said softly as he leaned in and did just that...kissed me.

Kissing me.

It was a soft, introductory kiss. Maybe he sensed my confusion. Or maybe he was polite. Either way, it was a kiss that didn't demand anything. It just said, this-could-be-good.

In other words, it was the perfect first kiss.

"Another example of do-it-then-apologize-after?" I asked as I grinned. I knew I was grinning because my cheek muscles hurt from trying to move my cheeks higher than normal.

It had been a long time since I'd kissed a man and my cheek muscles were obviously very happy about it.

"It wasn't much of a kiss. Do I need to apologize?" Micah was grinning as well and didn't look the least bit apologetic.

I shook my head. "No. No, I don't think you do."

"Good. Next time I kiss you, I'll do better."

For a moment, I thought he might kiss me again.

For a moment, I thought I might kiss him.

But neither of us did. He said, "I'd better get going. I have to be in court tomorrow at eight a.m. Try not to get in any trouble tomorrow while I'm tied up."

"I'll try," I teased.

"And call the detective," he said again.

I nodded.

I walked him down the front stairs, unlocked the door at the bottom and stood there awkwardly. After that kiss, I didn't know what to expect. I didn't know what I wanted to happen.

"Good night," he said. I heard him murmur, "Millie," then laugh as he got in the car and pulled away.

I realized at that moment, as I watched him walk away, that I had known precisely what I'd wanted.

I'd wanted another kiss.

Millie was his sister.

Despite the lack of the second, better follow up kiss he'd alluded to, the first one and knowing that Millie was his sister was enough to make me smile as I went back inside.

***

I tossed and turned that night. I woke up, made a giant pot of coffee and before I went downstairs, I called the detective.

"Yes," she barked in the phone when they connected me.

I felt awkward enough about the call and her salutation—or lack thereof— didn't help. She annoyed me.

Maybe it was the restless night.

Maybe it was that I hadn't finished my coffee.

Either way, I snapped back. "I've been doing some research—"

"If you're impeding my investigation, I'll charge you with impeding an investigation."

"That was a redundant sentence," I said testily, then added, "I would love to see you take that charge to the DA and make it stick. I'd love to see you try to explain how my running Internet searches could impede anything. Maybe if you feel the need to charge me with something, you could make a better case for *willful research.* I wonder how the DA would react to that? Let me know. Now do you want to hear what I've found?"

She sighed. "What did you find?"

"No answers," I assured her. "Just more questions. Junior's father is in prison. He pleaded guilty."

"Yes. I know that," she snapped.

I was beginning to think snapping was her normal conversational style.

I took a sip of coffee, trying to drown my annoyance. "But did you know the judge almost didn't accept his plea?"

"No," Detective Dana said slowly.

"Senior tried to plead guilty with qualifications. *Guilty But* isn't a permissible plea and the judge firmly told him that, so he finally pleaded just guilty."

"I don't see what that matters," she said.

"It matters because afterward, he was overheard saying he knew who rolled on him and he blamed them. He said, 'He'll get his.'"

"And you think he suspected his own son of rolling on him and had him killed?" she asked.

"No. I don't know. But it could mean something," I said. I wasn't going to outline my collecting information style of research. I didn't feel the need to tell her that sometimes when I was preparing a contract or even writing a report back in school, those random facts took on unimaginable significance.

As a detective, I felt she should be able to see the merit of collecting information to further a case.

Since she didn't seem to, I felt a little less sure of her abilities.

"Or it could be a fence pleaded guilty and when he was on his way to jail he simply blew off steam," she said.

"Yes, it could mean that too." I took a deep breath and then added, "Listen, I wouldn't have bothered you, but Micah insisted."

"Now you listen, I know you're vested in this investigation—"

I interrupted her. "Yes, I am. Someone broke into my house, even if you didn't find any evidence of that. They came in uninvited and burned a body in my kiln. They burned up someone I knew. Which means, even if you don't think I did it, I'm a suspect. So, yeah, you can bet that I'm invested."

She sighed loudly this time. "Invested or not, leave the investigating to me. It's my job. And I'm good at my job."

This time it was my turn to sigh. "I hope so," is all I said.

I didn't promise not to continue researching. "I should also mention that the guy who used to own this house and lost it to the bank is in jail." There were a lot of people with questionable lifestyles who kept turning up in this case, I thought but didn't say. What I did say was, "His wife uses her maiden name again, Trisha Jenkins, and works as a bartender at *Down By the Bay*."

"You have been busy," Detective Dana said with absolutely no appreciation in her voice. No, I was pretty sure her tone was annoyance.

"Yes, I have been busy," I agreed as if she had been complimenting me. "Her ex is in prison for theft and she gave me a list of everyone else they gave keys to. Her mom, his mom, and my neighbor, Miss Betty, who we knew about because I gave her a key, too."

"Wait, you went to see her?" The detective was obviously not as slow as I thought.

"Yes," I admitted.

"Listen, you can't go poking around. What if you stumble across the murderer? You could get hurt."

This was the first time anyone had confirmed it was murder. "So, it was someone covering up a murder?"

"I didn't say that," she said quickly.

Too quickly.

I had another Post-It to add to my board. "But you didn't say *illegally disposing of a corpse*, you said, *murderer*."

"Sometimes your inner lawyer shows through." This was very snarky. And still annoyed.

"Listen, I just went to the bar and had a drink and happened to talk to Trisha." Then I added, "Micah was with me."

I didn't add he came in later.

"No more talking to anyone who is even remotely tied to this case," she said, warning in her tone now.

"You've made yourself clear on that," I said, not agreeing to her ultimatum. "I've got to go. I'm going to finish my order today. I just want it all fired and packed up."

"In a new kiln?" she asked.

"Yes. I'm never using that dead-body kiln again."

She chuckled and hung up.

I realized that chuckle made her sound almost human. It was still an awkward phone call.

But I'd kept my promise to Micah.

I wondered when I'd see him again so I could say as much.

**

The rest of the day, as well as the next, were busy. I finished throwing my production order and would need to fire one more kiln of bisque cups and bowls to be able to deliver it.

But it was done.

It was a huge weight off my shoulders. I celebrated Wednesday night by starting a new ceramic sculpture. I decided to try something bigger than normal. A new version of *Dryad Emerging*.

I decided to try for something three feet.

And I tried to ignore all the gawkers that Adi was dealing with.

I concentrated on my work.

I sculpted the tree one piece at a time. Letting one section dry out enough to support the weight of the next section.

Piece by piece it grew. I worked on the table that was visible from the shop through the window.

"People are fascinated by your work," Adi said. "You might need to get some more pieces done for me. We're going through our stock more quickly than normal."

I nodded. I could sit down at the wheel and throw more pieces for the shop, but the new sculpture was weighing on my mind.

Maybe it was serving as a distraction. I needed something to keep me from thinking about how my life had changed just one week ago.

After we closed the shop and I told Adi goodnight, I picked up Miss Betty for our weekly trip to the grocery store.

"How are you?" she asked as I drove to Wegman's on upper Peach Street.

"Good," I answered, though that wasn't quite true. *Better* would have been closer, but I decided not to worry about the distinction. I wanted to see if my feelings about Trisha were accurate, so I said, "I ran into someone you know."

"Who?" she asked.

"Trisha, who used to own my house." I watched her expression.

She smiled. "Oh, she was always so nice. Now, that husband of hers wasn't. The man was rude from day one. They were always mismatched."

"He's in jail now," I said, wondering why so many people in this were involved with the law. From lawyers, to crooks. This situation had all the angles covered.

"Trisha divorced her husband," I added.

"Good for her," Miss Betty said with a bit more enthusiasm than was required. "She deserves better."

As I parked, I realized that if Trisha's ex was a thief, he probably had to do something with the things he stole. Maybe use a fence like Senior? If so, that was a connection, though I wasn't sure what the connection could mean since both Senior and Tyler were locked up.

Still, I filed the thought away. I'd add it to my board later.

This entire situation was like a big jigsaw puzzle. Each piece added something to the whole, even if it was something insignificant.

Miss Betty and I went to Wegman's café for dinner before we started our shopping. We both got sushi. Over the last year, we'd been working on using chopsticks. We were still not experts, but most of the time we both managed to get our food to our mouths.

Tonight, I had spicy shrimp sushi with veggie dumplings on the side.

I almost had a dumpling to my mouth when I inelegantly dropped it.

We both burst out laughing, even though it wasn't really that funny.

"Practice makes perfect," Miss Betty said as she expertly plopped a bite into her mouth.

We finished our dinner and our shopping and headed home.

This.

This was normal.

This was my simple, normal, everyday life.

I knew it was just a reprieve, but I relished it. I appreciated it. I was pretty sure the respite was going to help me get through the less-than-normal part...namely, who killed Junior Summers and why did they put his body in my kiln?

Chapter Ten

*"Sometimes you need to figure out
what doesn't work with your pottery
before you can figure out what does."*
Harry's Pottery: A Personal Journey

I bagged up my new Dryad tightly so she wouldn't dry out and worked on some new thrown pieces on Friday.

Adi still had a brisk business out front and my inventory was going down rapidly. I was chomping at the bit to work on the new piece, but as a small business owner, I knew I had to take advantage of the uptick in customers.

I tried not to think about the reason for the uptick, but that was hard, since I spent the better part of my day staring at my idea wall.

Senior was in prison for fencing stolen items.

He knew who rolled on him, he'd said.

He wanted revenge.

The previous owner of my house, Tyler Tawny was in prison theft.

Did he use Senior as a fence?

Even if he did, what did that have to do with anything? Tyler was still locked up, so he didn't kill Junior.

Junior had gone to school with me.

He'd danced with me at the prom.

He was fired in my kiln by someone with enough knowledge of kilns to start it, but not to understand that it takes hours to ramp up the temperature.

There was no evidence of someone breaking in.

It was probable that someone had a key.

A lot of people had keys.

Like my wheel, my thoughts kept going round and round. Spinning from one random fact to another.

All were pieces of this puzzle, but so far, nothing seemed to fit together.

I was no closer to an answer.

Adi came back after she turned the sign to closed and locked the front door.

"It's been a crazy week," she said. "You're really going to need more stock."

"I have a bit more in the store room and I'm starting some new kitchenware. I have that new glaze I experimented on. It'll look great," I said, hoping I sounded chipper about the work rather than frustrated about random facts that wouldn't fit together.

"Thanks for the extra hours," she said.

Normally I'd be hesitant about spending the extra money, but with the increased sales, I felt justified. I needed to make more stock more than I needed to deal with curiosity seekers.

"Thanks for the help. I know you generally only pick up a few days here and there, but if you're willing to work a bit extra next week, I'll take any days you can spare."

She grinned. "I love that working from home means I can be with Nori and work my schedule around her, but it's so nice to be out with real adults sometimes. So I'm happy to take extra hours when I can. Let me check with Mom and I'll text you a schedule."

I felt a surge of relief. "Great."

Adi paused and asked, "Are you really okay?"

I nodded. "Well, almost okay. I was out with Miss Betty last night and realized that it almost felt normal. That's what I want...just to get back to normal. I don't think I really appreciated how much I love this new life I've built until now. The *Wine and Mud* ladies will be here soon. It will be another step towards normal."

Adi laughed. "I've met your *Wine and Mud* class. They are anything but normal."

We both cracked up. The ladies were normal, in that they were very individual, but came together for these classes without worrying about their differences.

"Truth," I said with a smile. "But I can't picture any of them breaking in here to burn a body."

I expected Adi to wholeheartedly concur, but instead she asked, "But they did have a key?"

I sighed. "Yes. I'm sure the detective has talked to them by now."

"Maybe you should cover the board up?" She pointed to my board.

"I'm already set." I'd attached an old sheet to the top of the board, rolled it up and tied it above my idea board. I climbed a chair and let it drop down in place. "Ta da."

"Do you think they'll ask what's under it?" she asked.

I slid my small worktable in front of the curtain, then gently carried my dryad and placed it on top. "I'll just tell them I'm working on something new to surprise them."

Adi nodded her approval. "That should do it." She glanced at her watch. "I've got to run. I'll be here in the morning."

"Bring Nori. I've got my kids' class and you know she loves it. Plus I've got her birds ready to go."

"All I've heard about is her cards," Adi said with a laugh. "And of course she loves the class. Between you and the other kids, she's the center of attention. She loves that."

I laughed. "Everyone should feel they're the center of attention from time to time." My laughter died as I realized that I was the center of attention with the body and I wasn't finding it a very positive experience.

"See you tomorrow," Adi said and left.

I made sure the door was locked and headed upstairs for a quick meal. I munched on my spinach omelet and wished Micah had done the cooking. My omelet was more of scrambled eggs because it fell apart.

I was frowning at my inelegant plate when my phone rang. It was Micah.

"I was just thinking about you," I said, without thinking. I didn't want him to think he was at the center of my thoughts.

And when he said a long, drawn out, "Oh?" with a tone that said that's exactly what he thought, I clarified, "I was eating my version of an omelet."

"Which is?"

"Scrambled eggs."

He laughed. "I would have cooked for you."

"I don't think that's part of your attorney job description. It was never part of mine," I said, reminding both of us that whatever this was between us wasn't normal.

"No but cooking for you is a good way for a guy to see you in a non-lawyer way. And just to be clear, the guy in question is me."

I realized I was grinning like a loon and was thankful he couldn't see me. As if he'd heard my thoughts, he said, "When can I see you again?"

"I have class tonight and then tomorrow morning. We close the shop at three."

"I could tempt you with dinner tomorrow night?" he asked.

Part of me thought I should say no. I'd spent way too much time with Micah since we met. I'd spent even more time thinking about him. But instead of the word *no*, the other part of me said, "You don't need to tempt me. How about we go out to eat? My treat," I offered.

I was surprised by how very much I wanted to see him. I missed him.

"You don't—" he started.

I interrupted. "It's my way of saying thank you for all the non-lawyer stuff you've done."

"Not necessary, but yes" he said. "I'll pick you up at five?"

"Sounds great. I can't wait." At that moment, my phone flashed that someone was ringing my new doorbell. "I think my class is here. I'll see you tomorrow."

"I can't wait," he said, then hung up.

I shoved the last bit of my omelet in my mouth and hurried downstairs. My class had arrived en masse. "Come on in," I said, opening the door for them.

Barbara Ann, Charlotte, Liz, and Helen came in.

"Julie's coming, but she's running late," Barbara Ann said.

The four of them walked through the shop to the studio. I had a shelf in the back that they left their work on, along with aprons and tools.

They got their work out of tightly sealed bags, which kept the clay from drying out, and took their seats. I got out my new dryad and sat down to work with them.

"Oh, Harry, that's going to be amazing," said Barbara Ann. "Is it going to be like the other one?"

"Like, but not the same. I sold that first one," I added nonchalantly, though I felt anything but nonchalant. I was practically bursting with pride that it sold.

"Where's Julie?" I asked.

"Just running late because her husband's running late," Helen said.

"Men," Barbara Ann scoffed. She'd divorced her husband last year and was a bit bitter since, not that I blamed her.

And I thought about Micah. "Some men are sweet."

They all stopped.

I could feel myself smiling. My expression gave me away.

"Spill," Char said. She was the oldest one in the class, but if I had to pick someone who could carry a grown man into my studio and toss him in a kiln, it would be Char. She was a sturdy woman.

At that moment she gave me such a warm look that I felt immediately guilty for the thought.

I couldn't find a way to believe anyone in my *Wine and Mud* class could do anything like that.

The doorbell rang. "I'm literally saved by the bell," I said as I wiped my hands on my apron and got to the door.

Julie held a larger than usual bag aloft. "The wine has arrived," she said merrily. "I doubled down on the wine. After your last week, I figured a couple glasses each was called for."

"You can say that again," I agreed.

Like the others, Julie was at home in my studio. She set the bottles and paper cups on the table...we didn't use real wine glasses because everything in the studio got covered with clay. It was easier to just toss the cups. She got her project and took her seat.

"Have we started talking about the elephant in the room?" Julie asked, taking a sip of wine.

"Not yet," said Char. "Harry was just going to tell us about her new man. I thought that would ease us into talking about...well, you know."

I did know and so did everyone else.

"I know that the detective probably wanted to talk to all of you and I'm so sorry," I said.

"Harry," Julie scolded. "You have absolutely nothing to be sorry for. Frankly, my girls were in awe of how cool I've become. It seems no one else in class had a mom who was interviewed by the cops about a murder. Two teens and a preteen think I'm cool. I have you to thank for that."

I knew she was trying to find a silver lining. That was Julie. If you gave her a blemished apple, she'd make applesauce.

She grew a bit more serious. "But how are you?"

"Better, I think," I said. "There's a new security system and the detective hasn't been knocking on my door for a bit, so..." I shrugged.

"I didn't make a copy of the key," Julie said, all serious.

"I never, not for a moment, thought you did. I had to give your name because you all came in and used it, but I..." I shook my head again.

Char flexed the muscle in her arm. "Now we all know I could toss a body with the ease of a Scottish man tossing a caber, but Barbara Ann couldn't. No way. I told the detective as much. I told her about my Cross Fit class. I may have another convert."

Char had tried to get me to go to her Cross Fit class. I knew it came from a place of love. But I'd watched a video online and decided my daily walks—my *almost* daily walks—were good enough for me.

Liz smiled. "The detective was very polite. The twins were impressed, too. They wanted to know if they could come to class tonight. I think they thought they could solve the murder themselves. I told them leave it to the cops."

I'll confess, I cast a guilty look at my idea wall. No one had commented on the cover.

Liz was still talking. "I said this was a no kid zone. I said that students had to be at least twenty-one for this class because of the wine. Yes, I blamed the wine." She laughed.

Helen smiled indulgently at Liz.

Helen was an attorney. She was the only one here who had any legal knowledge. She'd have known that the kiln was a good way of getting rid of trace evidence. Still, no matter how I twisted it, I couldn't figure out how she'd have gotten the key from Julie and why she'd kill someone. "Someone knew a bit about kilns. Obviously, we all do. You've let us help load them. But, as I told the detective, having a bit of knowledge isn't the same as having a motive. I've never met this Steve Summers."

The rest of the group murmured their me-eithers.

I didn't me-either. Neither did I say, *I knew him.* I concentrated on my sculpture and tried not to feel guilty, as if I were lying to friends.

The rest of the class went well. I helped Helen with using the extruder to make coils. We talked about how to add new coils onto a piece.

It was almost nine before they all left.

Helen, the ADA, whispered, "If you are interviewed, take an attorney. Okay?"

"I've got one." She nodded, satisfied.

Julie was the last one out the door. "Are you really okay?" she asked with such concern I felt myself tear up.

"I keep telling myself it is what it is. I didn't do it and I trust the legal system will find the real killer. But..."

"Yes. But." She gave me a very motherly hug.

Most of the time I didn't realize how much I missed my mother. She'd been gone more of my life than she'd been a part of it. But moments like this made me miss her so much it hurt. She'd have hugged me like Julie and told me everything would be all right, and because she was my mother, I'd believe her.

"If you need anything, call. I mean it," Julie said.

I believed her. "I will."

"Listen, they spent a lot of time asking me about the key I borrowed. I told them no one else in class had access to it and I just kept it for those couple days. I returned it that Sunday. I can't imagine why they'd think I did it, but I didn't know him and I have no motive. Should I get an attorney?"

I knew she was asking me as an attorney, not as a potter. I nodded. "If they call you to question you again, yes. Not that I think you did anything or think they think you did anything. It's just that having an attorney with you is an insurance policy. I'm sorry that this mess is affecting you."

"Ditto."

"I really don't think you're in any danger though. Here's the name of a friend." Brenda used to work for my father but had left to start a small firm with her friend, Cindi Warren. "If they call you again, call her and tell her I recommended her to you.

She took the piece of paper. "Thanks, I will."

"But I don't think they will."

After she left, I closed, locked, and double checked the locks on the door, then went back to my studio. I moved the table out and rolled the fabric up off my idea board.

Did I learn anything tonight?

No. I didn't think any of my *Wine and Mud* moms did it. Julie would have been the most likely candidate, but no matter how I tried, I just couldn't picture her making a copy of the key—that would have shown premeditated intent. I thought anyone could kill someone if the circumstances were right. I mean, to save a child?

I didn't have kids, but I thought of Nori and if someone were hurting her, I'd do anything to save her.

But to plan it out? I simply couldn't see Julie doing that.

So no, I didn't learn one darned thing.

Now what?

***

I tossed and turned all night. I alternated worrying about Junior and worrying about an official date with Micah.

One was a horrible sort of worry.

Nightmares about Junior in my kiln, dressed for prom, and glowing from the heat as he asked me to dance.

The other was a good sort of worry. Eating dinner with Micah. Kissing Micah.

It had been a long time since I'd dreamed about a man.

Maybe my divorce had messed me up more than I thought.

Or maybe I'd been waiting for the right man.

Either way, despite everything that was going on, I couldn't stop thinking about Micah.

That might explain why I was groggy the next morning when I let Adi into the shop with Nori in tow.

I hadn't given Adi a new key. I hadn't given anyone but my father a new key. I felt nervous about allowing anyone to have access to my place.

Every time I thought about that, I felt angry about whoever it was who'd robbed me of my peace.

Then I felt guilty as I realized that robbing me of my peace wasn't nearly as bad as robbing Junior of his life.

"Hi, Aunt Harry. I'm gonna make a Knuffle Bunny today," the four-year-old announced.

I looked up at Adi, not sure what Nori was talking about. She had remarkably clear speech for a four-year-old, but sometimes things came out a bit garbled.

Adi smiled. "Nori's new passion. Mo Willem's Knuffle Bunny books."

I shook my head, indicating I didn't have a clue.

Adi just laughed. "You will know all about them before the end of the day."

And I did.

So did all the older kids who arrived for their ten a.m. *Clay Play* class. Unlike last night, I didn't need to weigh and measure each of the kids for possible motives for putting Junior in my kiln. Lynn, Patti, Kathi, Britta, and Brenda were exactly who and what they were. They were kids having fun with clay. And they knew all about Knuffle Bunny before their time was up.

At the end of the two hours, the kids wrapped up any projects from the week before and the five big kids as well as Nori had bunnies for the kiln. I promised to fire them to bisque before next week's class.

"Can I come again?" Nori asked.

"You are always welcome," I said.

When the big girls left, Nori and I had lunch and then she settled down for a nap on the couch in the back corner by the kitchenette.

I'd covered my Idea Board when the kids had come.

I uncovered it now and studied it as I worked.

I was no closer to an answer.

I got up and wrote, *What Am I Missing?* in the center of the board.

There were no signs of a break in. Oh, maybe someone had picked the lock, but I'd had deadbolts. I imagined those would be harder to pick than a handle lock.

Occam's Razor said the simplest solution was generally the right one.

In that case, someone with a key had broken in.

One previous owner was in jail.

The other didn't strike me as someone who'd murder someone then break into my place to burn up the body.

That was the problem. No one who had access to a key struck me as someone who'd murder someone.

I wiped my clay-covered hands on my apron and got back up and underneath *What Am I Missing?* I wrote *Who Am I Missing?*

I was pretty sure that question was the answer.

Who.

Someone I hadn't discovered yet was the murderer.

Someone who had access to a key or access to someone who had access to a key.

I took my chalk and put large X's through everyone's name on my board.

I was pretty sure that I knew who the murderer wasn't...none of the above.

Now I just had to figure out who the murderer was.

I'd start with the person I knew the least.

Trisha.

I knew where I was taking Micah to dinner tonight.

Chapter Eleven

*"Mugs and cups are always a
popular item for a working potter."*
~Harry's Pottery: A Personal Journey

I sipped my beer from the glass.

"This would be nicer from an old-fashioned beer stein. I've made a few back at my place. I'll make you a drink in one sometime," I said.

We were sitting at the bar. Trisha was indeed working and greeted us as if we were old friends.

Micah kept shooting me looks that I ignored as I sipped my beer. I was thinking about a children's song, *Down By the Bay* and thinking it would be a cute marketing campaign for the bar. A llama in pjs. A whale with dots on her tail...

I could do a series of steins...

Micah interrupted my beer stein thoughts. "Okay, why are we here?"

I answered semi-honestly. "I was just thinking about how I could make some steins—"

"Harry..."

I sighed. "I promised to take you out and I heard their steak and avocado salad was to die for," I tried. "That's what I'm getting. And they've got some local beers on tap. This BREWtal Erie beer is worth the visit. I loved that they're capitalizing on Erie's crazy winter."

Last winter had been a record breaker. I don't remember ever shoveling so much snow. We were becoming known for our local breweries and I was particularly in love with this new seasonal stout named after the event. There'd been a big write up in the paper yesterday about it.

"I read the article too and—"

I pretended I didn't know Micah was about to scold me. "I love that we have so many local breweries and—"

"Harry," he said in a tone that indicated he wasn't buying my explanation.

"Fine," I said, admitting defeat. "I was asking myself what I was missing last night, then I realized the question wasn't what, but who. *Who* am I missing? I just can't figure out why anyone on my list would kill Junior, much less stuff him in my kiln. And if it's not one of them, then it's someone I haven't found yet. Trisha seemed like the most likely place to start."

"You think she did it?" he asked, eyeing the friendly bartender who was down at the other side of the bar.

"No. But I'm wondering about her husband. He's in jail for theft and burglary. Senior was known to fence stolen merchandise and he's in jail. Junior took over the legit business when his father went away. What if he took over the illegitimate business, too? I don't believe in coincidences. Two of these people are locked up. It seems like it should be an intersection of some kind. I just can't figure out what. But since they're locked up, we know they didn't do it. The question is, who am I missing?"

"And there's the whole, someone needed to know you have a kiln and have at least a cursory understanding of how it works," Micah said.

"You can Google that much. And they didn't know enough because they used a programmed setting that didn't get nearly hot enough. If they'd totally destroyed the bones, we wouldn't know who the victim was. So, it's a good thought. But they didn't know enough for it to work."

Trisha brought our dinners and I thanked her. I wondered how I could ask her about her ex without alienating her.

I took a bite and realized coming for dinner had been a great idea, even without talking to Trisha. "This is fantastic," I said. Micah took a bite of his mushroom burger and nodded his agreement.

We ate and I tried to think about less controversial topics. I started with the new sculpture.

I asked Micah about people I knew at the firm. Not in a gossipy way, but in a common-ground way.

I was nearing the end of my salad and still had no idea how to broach the subject of her ex with Trisha, but I was saved when she came down to us during a lull. "I know our food's marvelous, but I suspect you wanted to ask something else."

She had no problem coming right out and asking, so I did the same. "Could your ex have given anyone else a copy of your key?"

"He was not the brightest bulb in the pack, so yes. I can tell this is freaking you out. Why don't I call him?" she offered kindly.

I knew I'd liked Trisha and that feeling was reinforced. "You'd do that?"

She nodded. "Listen, part of whatever he's done is my fault. I should have seen him for what he was from the get-go. All I can say is sometimes love blinds, and even more importantly, sometimes love is just lust."

I thought of Alex, and of Adi and her ex. I nodded. "You can say that again."

"I'll call and see what he says. I wanted to come check out the shop anyway. I'll bring you the news," she offered.

"And when you do, I have an idea for your boss here. I'll do a couple drawings and if you like them, maybe you can show the owner."

She smiled. "Great."

We went back to our meal when Trisha moved down the bar.

"Feel better?" Micah asked.

I shrugged. "I'm just wondering about all the people I'm connected to who've been arrested or are in jail. Not that I know Trisha's ex or Junior's dad, but there's a connection. It makes me uncomfortable."

"I think as attorneys we sort of sign on to associate with criminal elements. It's part of the job description."

"I'm a potter now. It's not part of my description any more. And frankly, it never was. I handled a few cases in court, but I did more contract work. Contracts don't have much to do with criminals."

Micah laughed, as if what I said was funny. But truly, I didn't intend it to be. As an attorney, my job was to protect my client's interests. I did that through writing and vetting contracts. I think part of the reason I never did much criminal law was that I didn't want to defend unsavory sorts.

I certainly didn't intend to start dealing with them as a potter.

We finished our meal and walked along the bayfront sidewalk, admiring the view.

During the summer, the bay would be awash with boat lights, but most of the boats had gone to their winter homes and the only lights came from the Presque Isle peninsula.

In the winter—at least on winters that were cold enough for the bay to ice over—the bay would be filled with fishing shacks. But this time of year, it seemed quiet and solitary. There was a cool northerly breeze blowing across the lake. I wrapped my arms around myself, wishing I'd brought a jacket.

Micah put his arms over my shoulders. "It's getting brisk out."

I snuggled in closer. I was warmer, but I don't think it had to do with him sharing body heat as much as...well, heat.

How is it I felt this close to someone I'd known for such a short time?

Tonight was our first official date.

The last time I'd felt this way about someone, it was Alex. I'd fallen head-over-heels fast and hard.

I didn't want to make that mistake again.

Sure, there were sparks between Micah and me.

That was good. I hadn't sparked at all since Alex and I split. It was as if I'd locked away a part of myself after my divorce and that part was now coming back to life.

Yes, that was good, but I didn't want to make the same mistake for a second time.

I pulled away from Micah slightly, though I didn't totally break free from his arms. "I like you," I blurted out.

"I like you, too," he said.

I started, "But—"

"Uh, oh," he said. "Nothing good ever comes after a woman says the word *but*."

I smiled. "I don't think it's too bad a *but*. I just want to be clear. I'm divorced and afterwards, I was so tied up with getting my business off the ground I haven't thought about dating or anything else. And I had fun tonight. I've had fun all the other nights we just hung out. But I don't want to move too fast. I just want..."

I didn't know how to finish that. I just wanted Micah, but not yet. "I..."

"Slow and steady," he said. "I don't have any expectations. I really just like spending time with you. So right now, we won't even call what we're doing dating. We're two potential friends who enjoy each other's company and are getting to know each other better. We're not labeling things any more than that."

I shot him a wry smile. "Which is wise because that's a lot to fit on a label."

He laughed and then grew more serious. "I've been out of dating circles myself. This new job for your father has been all I can handle. I get it."

"No ex lurking in your past?" I couldn't help but ask.

Micah knew at least that much of my past and I greedily wanted to know about his.

He answered me slowly. "I think we all have an ex lurking in our pasts. Not an ex-wife for me, though."

I could sense that was all he wanted to say on that matter for now. I didn't blame him. Talking about ex's wasn't a great way to end our non-date.

We walked quietly down my street and stopped on my porch.

"I think this is where we say goodnight," he said. "I know we agreed we'd be taking things slow and that we're just potential friends, but does that mean I can make a request?"

"You can always ask," I hedged. Something in the way he phrased his sentence told me I wasn't going to be happy about this request.

He nodded. "If you decide to go talk to other people about what happened, take me along. And before you bristle and call me a sexist or tell me I'm not your father—something I know and I'm eternally grateful for—let me assure you that it's because two people nosing around are safer than one. That's why so many cops have partners. Everyone needs someone who will have their back."

I had indeed been about to bristle, so his observation was spot on. And what he'd said made sense. "I won't promise to never go anywhere without you, because I can't foresee every possible twist and turn in the future, but I will promise that if at all possible, I'll take you."

He looked like he was going to argue, so I added, "I take my promises seriously. And I truly try to never break one. I can't make such a unilateral blanket promise, but I will try...that I can promise wholeheartedly."

He sighed. "I guess that's enough for me then."

I smiled. "I don't think we've clarified how two taking-it-slow, potential-friends say goodnight." I stood on tiptoe and kissed his bristly cheek. "I thought this might do."

He leaned down and kissed my cheek as well. I could smell his cologne. Or maybe he just naturally smelled of something warm and spicy. The scent made me think of a forest after a rain. A place that was quiet, peaceful, and safe.

And for a moment, I wanted to forget about taking things slow, even though I'd been the one to suggest it.

Before I could change my mind, I said, "Goodnight."

My voice sounded husky to my ears.

"Goodnight," he said as well. "Is calling tomorrow allowable while we're taking things slow?"

"Calling tomorrow would be lovely. I'll talk to you then."

I unlocked my handle and deadbolt. Micah waited until I was inside and I clicked the deadbolt back in place. I watched through the small window as he turned and walked away from the porch.

Taking things slowly made sense.

I'd only known Micah a week and a half. I didn't want to rush things. I didn't want to hurry things.

I wanted to be sure that what I felt for him wasn't just some reaction to the trauma of finding a body in my kiln and finding myself under police investigation.

I didn't think it was, but then I suspect no one who finds their feelings influenced by circumstances thinks that's what happening.

I was sensible.

Slow and steady.

Those were my watch-words.

But as I turned and went up the stairs to my apartment, I wish I wasn't so sensible.

***

The week went by with a more normal flow.

Adi came in Tuesday, but customers had fallen to a slower paced, normal level. I could handle things myself, so she was going to work Friday and Saturday, which was also normal.

I got the paper from the front porch on Wednesday morning and waved at Hap, which was my normal rhythm. He walked to work every day and waving at him was part of my routine.

I'll confess, it felt good to be back to it.

The only new addition to my week was Micah's daily phone calls. He was busy with the new case and we agreed we'd see each other on Saturday after I closed the shop.

On Friday, I left Adi at the shop and walked back to *Ember and Forge* for a coffee after lunch. This too was part of my routine. A nice break in the afternoon when Adi was there to cover the shop before I had my *Wine and Mud* ladies Friday nights.

I mulled over my stalled Idea Board.

I hadn't had any new ideas.

Trisha had stopped by this morning and bought a mug. She said she'd talked to her ex and he had no new names of people with keys.

I was stalled.

I just hoped that Detective Dana was making progress, though I hadn't heard a peep from her either.

I didn't have much experience as a suspect in a homicide, or at least a kiln-cremation, but I guess keeping suspects apprised of your investigation wasn't a cop priority.

I'd covered my board before I left in anticipation of tonight's *Wine and Mud* and tomorrow's *Clay Play*.

I decided to give myself a break from it as well. I'd uncover the board Sunday and mull some more.

Maybe a couple days away would stir some ideas.

I walked into the coffee shop and ordered my usual house blend, large.

Go big or go home was my coffee motto.

I turned, ready to take my coffee and walk down by the bay but stopped. I was surprised to see Hap sitting in one of the plush chairs, his laptop appropriately on his lap and a coffee at hand.

I walked over and teased, "Hey, what're you doing here in the middle of the day? Playing hooky?"

Rather than laughing, which I expected, Hap looked guilty.

Very guilty.

"What's up?" I asked.

He nodded at the chair next to his and I sat down. "Hap?"

"Please, don't tell Kitty," he said. "She'll just worry."

Hap and Kitty were normally tied at the hip. I couldn't imagine one of them keeping something from the other. "Worry about what? What's going on?"

Hap sighed, took a fortifying sip of his coffee and said, "I lost my job three months ago. Kitty's been so anxious about her job, I didn't want to tell her. I've got a lead on a new one and I'm still getting unemployment, so..."

I'm not sure what expression I was making. I suspect it was a combo of shock and anger.

Yes, anger.

You see, Hap and Kitty weren't just neighbors. They were a couple I thought had it all. They seemed to have everything Alex and I hadn't found with each other. They were a team. They were best friends. And they were palpably in love.

That's what I wanted next time.

Maybe Hap and Kitty were why I was taking things slowly with Micah. I wanted what they had. And I truly thought time was a way to allow that kind of relationship to grow.

That's a lot to put on someone else, even if they're not aware of it. And I felt guilty about it.

"Hap..." I started.

He hung his head, "I know. I know. I was downsized and I thought I could find something before I had to tell her. Then she wouldn't stress out. She's been so anxious about everything. Her work's been stagnating and she keeps worrying she'll be laid off. The day before I got my notice, she said that knowing one of us had a secure job was all that kept her going some days. Then they handed me my notice and..." Head hanging, he let his excuses die off.

"Hap. You have to tell her," I said gently.

"I know. I mean it, I know. Every day, I'm out stumping. I've had interviews and sent out a ton of resumes. Every day I tell myself that this is the day I'll get an offer and then I'll confess everything to her. We'll laugh about it and she'll be relieved because I'm working. And every day, nothing."

I didn't say anything because I didn't know what to say.

"I have to tell her," he said for me.

"You do. You two are a team. You can weather this," I said.

I believed it as I said it but couldn't help wondering if it was because I needed them to be able to weather it. And thinking that made me feel guilty all over.

"Thank you," he said.

For a moment, I wondered if Hap could lie to Kitty about getting fired and dress every day for *work* for months, what else was he capable of?

I tried to twist it every which way I could. He could have a key. He knew the Tawnys. Hap was able to heft a body. What he didn't have was a motive and I couldn't think of anyway a salesman would have motive.

No, I didn't think he did it, but I knew when I went home I'd put a small asterisks by his name. Just a reminder that even people we thought we knew could have secrets.

But for now, I shook off those thoughts and said, "Let's sit, drink our coffee, and forget about finding jobs and dead-body kilns."

"You know, you do fight unfairly." He laughed as he took a sip of coffee.

"How?" I asked, taking a sip of my coffee, needing it more than ever.

He all out smiled and said, "All I've got is this unemployment thing. I didn't find a body in a kiln."

I couldn't help it, I laughed. And then he laughed.

And I felt guilty for my doubting him.

***

After my coffee, I went back to my studio and threw three steins. I set them in front of the fan to dry, turning them frequently so they dried evenly. When they were leather-hard, I carved three verses from the children's song "Down by the Bay." A whale with dots on his tail. A llama in pjs. A moose and a goose.

The llama was the hardest one.

When I was done, I smiled. I painted the images with underglaze. After I fired them to bisque, I'd glaze the rest and put a clear glaze over the images.

I'd tried using glazes to paint with in the past, but I was never happy with the results. Glazes run.

Some run a lot.

Adi was suddenly in front of me and I realized I'd lost track of time. I couldn't help but smile. That was normal. I got lost in my work and huge chunks of time just disappeared.

"I'm closing up shop," she said. "It was a good day, but more back to normal good than last week."

I sighed. "I know I should be lamenting losing that influx of customers, but I don't."

"Me either, if I'm honest." She nodded towards the steins. "Those are cute."

"I've been down to *Down By the Bay* a few times lately and thought these would a great promotion. So many of the breweries around here have mug clubs. You buy into it and get a free beer once a week in your special mug. I thought these might work."

"They'd be promoting themselves and you'd be promoting your business. Make sure your logo goes on the bottom of each one," she said bossily.

I laughed. "I will, Mom."

She shook her head. "I didn't realize when I had Nori that my need to mother wouldn't be limited to her. I'll bring her with me tomorrow?" she half said and half asked.

"Of course. She loves *Clay Play*," I said, like I said every week.

"I just don't want to ever have you feel I'm presuming. I know she's a lot younger than the other kids you have in the class."

"Adi, let me be clear then, I adore your daughter. I mean, I'd do anything for her. So bringing her along will never be a problem. Part of the joy of owning the shop is I'm the boss and can run things the way I want. And I like having Nori around."

"You are the most amazing boss," she said. "And a good friend, and in that spirit, I should tell you that I've decided something."

"Oh?"

"I'm going back to school next year. I only need a few more credits to earn my degree." I knew that Adi didn't have a degree for the programming she did. She had a decent job, but with the proper initials after her name, she could have a better one. "Nori will be starting kindergarten, so I should have more time for classes. And I still really want to work here, but I wanted to let you know that my schedule might not be quite as flexible."

"That's fantastic," I said. "We'll make it work. Having you here at least a couple days a week gives me time to work. I don't think which day of the week matters. And you know if you need help with Nori, all you have to do is ask. She makes a great sidekick."

Suddenly, in spite of the fact I was covered with clay, Adi hugged me. "You are a great friend. I don't think I say that enough."

I was not a hugger by nature, but I hugged her back. "Me either, but you are."

I'd met Adi at *Ember and Forge.* I'd taken them a couple of my coffee mugs, suggesting they might want some. Adi had been getting a coffee as I spoke to the manager and she'd squealed when she saw them.

"I'd like my coffee in that," she said that first day.

I often thought Adi's enthusiasm had helped me make the sale.

After that, she'd visited the shop. She worked from home and felt her brain cells atrophying. I mentioned looking for someone for a few hours here and there, and...

The rest is history.

"Thank you," I said. I was thanking her for last week, but more than that, I was thanking her for all her support and even for that first day at the coffee shop.

"Right back at you. I don't know where I would have been without you supporting me through everything with Kev."

"You deserve better," I said. "You deserve the best." I thought about Barnabas and knew not only was he better, he was the best. I resolved to figure out ways to throw them together.

"You, too," she said.

"Well, this has become a huge love fest."

"We don't do it often, but I've learned that sometimes the words need to be said. See you tomorrow."

After Adi left, I locked up, took the day's receipts and put them in the small safe under the kitchenette's sink. I figured if anyone ever tried to rob me, that wouldn't be high on their list of places to look.

Who? I thought. That was the question I was missing.

I still thought it wasn't *what* I was missing, but *who.*

But maybe if I found out more *what*'s I'd find that *who?*

Chapter Twelve

*"There's a certain amount of
instinct in art.
Sometimes you try a new project
and innately realize something's missing.
I've learned to trust my gut when
that happens."*
~Harry's Pottery: A Personal
Journey

Friday night's *Wine and Mud* class
was normal.

I don't know that people realize
how nice normal is. At least not until they
lose their normal.

I'd lost mine and decided to
treasure every bit of normality that I
could eke out of my life.

Those were my thoughts Saturday
morning. I longed for another nice,
normal day. No more chaos. No more
confusion. Just a quiet, normal, everyday
day.

Adi brought Nori and the other
kids showed up at ten for the *Clay Play*
class. Britta asked if she could bring a
friend named Liz to the next class.

I said sure, but I was pretty sure
that would be the limit of kids I could
accommodate in one class. Maybe I'd have
to start a second class?

Nothing wrong with that.

I was smiling as we cleaned up for the day because Micah was coming over soon.

"You look like a cat who ate the canary," Adi said.

"I love cats," Nori said. "Are you gettin' a cat?"

"No," I said decisively. A cat would be a danger in the studio.

"I can't have one neither. But maybe a dog?" Nori eyed her mother.

Adi smiled. "I said maybe."

"There's a dog adoption event down at bayfront park today," I whispered to Adi, not wanting Nori to hear and pester her to death. "Barnabas told me about a grandmother who supposedly has a magic touch when it comes to matching people with the right dog."

Adi sighed even as she smiled. And I knew at that moment Nori was getting a dog today.

"Maybe we'll take a walk," she whispered back.

As they left at three that afternoon, I heard Adi say, "Let's not go home yet. Let's go look at the water."

Nori was enthusiastic about just going down to the bay. I could only imagine how happy she'd be looking at the dogs.

I grabbed a shower and put on non-work clothes. My work wardrobe consisted of jeans, t-shirts, and flannel shirts when the weather got colder. I didn't dress up much more than that for non-work events, but tonight I tried to be a step up from that. I put on *good* jeans, a blouse, and a sweater. I put on boots rather than sneakers.

It wasn't much, but it was better than most days.

I went hog-wild and actually used a bit of eyeliner.

I looked at the results in the mirror and hoped Micah noticed.

As if on cue, my doorbell rang. I didn't need to check my phone to know who it was.

Micah was waiting on the porch.

"Hi," he said.

"Hi," I said back, then laughed. We were two adults who'd spent an inordinate amount of time together lately. This shyness was uncalled for. "I sent Adi down to the bayfront with Nori. I wondered if you'd like to take a walk down and see if they got a dog at a dog fair down there."

"Sure. We can grab dinner afterward?" he asked.

"Sounds great." I could feel myself smiling. I tried to control it. I tried to play it cool, but it turns out I wasn't cool and I couldn't hide the fact I was happy to see him.

He smiled back, and we might not have known each other long, but I could see he was just as happy to see me. "You might want to grab a jacket. The wind's picking up. By the time we get out of dinner, it's going to be downright cold."

"Sure. Give me a sec. You can come up if you want."

"I'll just wait here. I want to enjoy every moment of decent weather we have left."

I didn't blame him. After last winter, the entire city was holding onto the good weather for as long as we could.

I ran up the stairs, grabbed a heavy jacket and tossed a hat and gloves in my pocket. I threw a wallet in my back pocket and my keys in my front pocket.

I sprinted back down the stairs. It wasn't that I was afraid Micah would leave, it was that I was anxious to be with him.

"There's a beauty to this time of year," he said as we walked. He took my hand. "The leaves are almost gone from the trees, but you can still spot some holdouts across the bay on the peninsula. And the geese are still gathering for their trip south. I love how they sound as they fly overhead. I've never decided if they're saying goodbye or calling others to join them."

"That was poetic," I said.

He laughed. "I wrote for our high school newspaper and won a poetry contest once. My mom was thrilled. My sister, Millie, taunted me for weeks. She still occasionally calls me Tennyson."

"Really? You won a poetry contest? You are a renaissance man."

He grinned and gave my hand another squeeze. "Coming from a renaissance woman, that's a compliment. I mean, you can write a contract and make a plate. That's truly renaissance."

I laughed, not because he'd said anything truly funny, but because I was happy.

Happy to be here with Micah.

Happy to be talking about things like poetry and plates.

Just happy.

Maybe some of that happiness stemmed from the fact he was still holding my hand.

We walked along the bay, weaving in front of and behind buildings until we reached the park. They had concerts here in the summer. I loved sitting on the bit of a hill, listening to music and watching the boats on the water as the sun set.

It was a little after four and the adoption day was due to end at five.

I looked among the makeshift kennels and spotted Adi and Nori. Nori's smile was visible from a distance. They stood in front of a long table near the bayside of the park.

I looked down and there was a tiny white dog on a lead next to her.

"I think she got her dog," I said as I hurried toward them.

"Aunt Harry, I've got a dog. Miss Muffet. Do you know the poem? Nana Vancy says it's 'cause she's got a patch of black on her back that looks like a spider. Get it?" The words spilled out, one after another, with no evidence of breathing in between any of them.

"I do know the poem," I smiled at Micah and mouthed the word Tennyson, then turned back to Nori and said, "She's lovely. May I say hi?"

"Oh, sure, she likes people. She's gonna sleep with me and eat breakfast with me and poop. Mom says I gotta help clean up her poop. That's gross, but when I was little my mom cleaned my poop diapers, so I guess I gotta do it for Miss Muffet." She finally took a breath and said, "Who's this?"

"This is my friend, Micah. Micah, this is my friend, Nori. And you're right, sweetie, we do have to take care of the people and dogs we love," I agreed.

Adi caught up to us and said, "I'm a soft touch."

I laughed and said, "You are."

"Mommy, this is Micah. He's Aunt Harry's friend, just like me."

At that moment a tiny old woman came up to us. "Who's here for the dog?"

I started to say neither of us, but she shook her head and said, "No, don't tell me. It's you. And I've been waiting for you," she told me.

"No, really, I can't," I said to thin air because the woman was already walking between the rows of makeshift kennels.

"Keep up," she called back over her shoulder.

One of the other older women behind the table said, "You'd better catch up."

"I will, if only to tell her I'm not taking a dog."

Micah chuckled.

I gave him the look I used on my *Clay Play* class when they got too wild. "I am not taking a dog and have no problems telling her so."

Which is why I hurried to catch up with the rather abrupt, older lady. She was kneeling at a cage. "Ma'am, I just wanted to say—"

"Lily, here's the lady I was telling you about. I know you've waited a long time to meet her." She turned to me. "This is her *third Everything But a Dog* day. I told her to be patient. That you were on your way, but *kedvenc,* you took your own sweet time getting here."

"What did you say her name was?" I asked as I knelt by the fencing that penned in the giant dog. As I knelt, she stood taller than my head. She was a light tan Irish Wolfhound, or at least a big part wolfhound.

"Lily," she said again.

I held out my hand and Lily daintily sniffed it, then licked it. I turned to the woman and said, "I'm Harry. I own Harry's Pottery up the way, which would make her..."

"Lily Potter," Micah said from behind me. "I think you're right, ma'am, Lily was destined to be Harry's dog."

"Or *she* was destined to be Lily's owner."

As if she heard us speaking, Lily gave a soft, woof.

"I want her, but I'm not sure how she'll do around the pottery," I said, trying to be practical. The shop was my business. My livelihood. If she became rambunctious and broke pieces, I could take a huge financial hit.

"She is the calmest dog I've ever seen. People think big dogs are more difficult, but I've found that they're basically just big carpets that need to go out for a walk on occasion."

Lily bumped my hand with her head and I knew she meant she needed pet, so I obliged.

"I..."

"Listen, if for some reason it doesn't work out, I'll take her," Micah said. "We'll make it work. It's obvious you're in love."

For a moment I wondered if he meant in love with Lily or with him. I knew he meant the dog. I knew it was too fast for any such emotion with him.

And yet, I'd fallen as hard for Micah as I had for Lily.

I heard myself saying, "I'll take her."

Which is why forty-five minutes later, Lily and I walked with Micah, Adi, Nori, and Miss Muffet back to my shop. Micah had gallantly suggested tonight might not be the best night for eating out and offered to go pick us up Thai food from my favorite place on the square.

Lily and Miss Muffet were sniffing my apartment with Nori following along when my phone rang.

I didn't recognize the number, so I held a finger up to Adi and went to the kitchen to take it.

"Hello?"

"I hear you've been investigating the body in your kiln," said a man's voice. It was low and gravely, as if he was trying to disguise it.

"Pardon," I said, trying to stop my knees from literally shaking and desperately wanting him to speak again. If he was trying to disguise his voice, then he must think I might recognize his voice.

"I don't know if you're doing it on your own or trying to help the cops, but either way, stay out of it. This is nothing to you," the voice said.

I didn't recognize the voice. Either he was very good at disguising it or he wasn't someone I knew well. But his assertion that this was nothing to me was wrong.

"You broke into my home and you tried to get rid of a body in my studio. It was my kiln," I said, feeling more angry than scared. "I didn't want to be involved, but you brought me into it. I'm a suspect."

"They'll figure out it wasn't you," he said.

"Yeah? What if they don't?" I asked.

"Stay out of this, Harry."

For a second there was something in his voice I thought I recognized. Something in the way he said my name. As if I'd heard him say it before. But for the life of me, I couldn't put my finger on it.

"Just get on with your life and forget about it. This is your only warning," the man said and then hung up.

I'd reread all the articles on Quincy Mac and I knew what she'd do. She'd try to figure out who was calling her with a warning.

I was not Quincy Mac.

I dialed the phone.

I was talking to Detective Dana when Micah walked in with two big paper bags of Thai takeout.

I hung up and filled him in before we went back out to the living room and called Adi and Nori to dinner.

I didn't say anything to them.

Adi was already worried enough.

Dinner was fun mainly because the dogs were a comedy act. Lily was very prim and proper. She didn't beg. Didn't pay the least bit of attention to our meal.

The dog group had sent them both home with food and Lily ate hers politely.

Miss Muffet, on the other hand, was not the least bit polite or proper. She gulped her food down with a speed that was amazing, then she begged for more. She did flips. She gnawed on Lily's ear and my new, giant dog simply batted the puppy away, which only made Miss Muffet more determined to gain Lily's attention.

"They're hysterical together," Adi said. "Although I think your dog's a bit more trained than ours."

"They said Lily's about four, so she's got a few years on Miss Muffet."

When we finished eating, Adi said, "I think we'd better head home. I'm not sure who's going to be more difficult to get to sleep, Nori or her dog."

"I'm gonna sleep good. Me and Miss Muffet are gonna be best friends," Nori announced.

"We'll see," Adi said with a grin that said even if Nori didn't sleep well, her mother wouldn't mind. "See you Thursday, unless you need me before."

"Things have slowed back down, so I think I'll be fine, but I'll call if that changes," I assured her.

"Don't go finding any more bodies in your kiln and I think you'll be fine," she joked. She must have seen my expression because she said, "Sorry, too soon."

"It's okay," I said, forcing a smile.

It wasn't too soon because of the body—it was too soon because the phone call that was freaking me out tonight.

After she left, I double-checked the door before I went back upstairs.

"Tell me again about the call?" Micah said.

Well, sort of commanded. I didn't take commands very well.

And maybe being annoyed was easier than being nervous. I snapped, "I called the detective. I'm fine."

Micah was astute enough to realize he'd overstepped. He said, "Sorry. It's just that I'm worried about you."

It was hard to be mad about that.

I sighed and told him. "It was a guy. I think he was purposefully trying to change his voice. He told me not to investigate the body. He said they were bound to figure out I didn't do it and it was none of my concern."

I didn't add that he'd told me this was my only warning.

"I believe I'm going to invite myself to spend the night," Micah announced.

"Micah, I'm fine," I assured him.

"I know. And I actually feel a lot better with you having a dog in the house, though Lily seems a little less than ferocious. Her size alone might convince an intruder to leave," he admitted.

"See, I'll be fine. Detective Dana said she'd stop by in the morning, unless something else happened tonight. I have her on speed dial," I said. I wasn't sure why I was fighting this so hard, because truth be told, I didn't relish the idea of being here alone after that call. Even with Lily serving as my bodyguard

"I'm still staying," Micah said. "I am not a man who tends to invite himself where he's not wanted, but Harry, I can't leave you alone after that call."

His concern for me was palpable. Rather than be swayed by that, I tried humor. "Listen, I know we've gone out, but I'm not that kind of a girl."

"On the couch," he assured me with a grin.

"What would my father say? He's your boss after all."

"I suspect he'd say thank you."

I sighed. "You're not making this easy."

"I'm not trying to. You and Lily can just go settle in. I'll be here until morning. If you play your cards right, I'll go get donuts at Mighty Fine Donuts for breakfast. And I'll make the coffee."

I admitted defeat, but to be honest, I was just as happy to have lost this particular argument. I did ask, "Apple fritters?"

"Yes."

"Fine. You can spend the night on the couch. You're lucky I have a huge couch despite the fact this is a small apartment. But it's just this one night."

"Deal." He held out his hand.

I took it and that sense of rightness that I'd felt when we held hands earlier swept over me again.

I pulled my hand away maybe a bit too abruptly and called my new dog. "Come on, Lily."

Lily was as polite that night as she was at dinner. She stood at the side of the bed asking permission and I said, "Sure. This is my side. That is your side."

She accepted my terms and got on the other side of the bed without complaint. She didn't stray on to my half as we slept, but I'll confess, I rolled closer to her and put my hand on her scruffy fur. I felt comforted.

I hadn't shared a bed with anyone since Alex.

And at that thought, I realized Micah was right outside my bedroom door, sleeping on my couch.

It would be easy to invite him into my bedroom.

But I liked Micah and didn't want to ruin what might be by rushing into something neither of us was ready for.

Okay, so maybe mainly what I wasn't sure *I* was ready for.

I settled for snuggling with Lily and tried to forget Micah was right outside my door.

***

I woke up the next morning to the smell of coffee.

As promised, there was a Mighty Fine Donut box in the center of the counter.

"How long have you been awake?" I asked as I glanced at the clock and realized it was only seven a.m.

"For a while. I stopped at my house and got a clean set of clothes. I borrowed your spare key so I could let myself back in. I hope you don't mind."

Despite not wanting to give too many people a key to my house, I didn't mind Micah using the spare.

"You brought me donuts, so why would I mind? I'll let Lily out then help myself."

"I've already had my first cup. I'll take her out," he offered.

"Thanks." I helped myself to a cup of coffee and an apple fritter.

I was thankful the backyard was fenced in. It would make having an impromptu dog easier.

Lily was quick. I heard her bounding up the stairs. I got up and fed her the last of the food the charity had sent home with her.

I was more than content as I ate my fritter and sipped my coffee.

Micah sat down next to me. "As long as you're in a good mood, I should probably let you know that I invited myself to brunch at your father's."

I sighed. "I won't complain that you're being a bit presumptuous if you promise not to mention the phone call last night. Detective Dana's supposed to be here around nine, it's all good. No need to bother my dad."

I'd have plenty of time to talk to her before heading to Dad's.

Micah looked a bit stubborn. "I think you should tell your father." He stared at me a moment, then added, "But I won't say anything if you don't want me to."

"I don't." I was sure about that. I wished I hadn't even said anything to Micah. There was nothing anyone could do but worry. "Did you tell him about Lily?"

"No," Micah said.

"Great. Then she'll be a surprise." We'd had a dog when I was growing up. I knew Dad loved animals and he wouldn't mind my bringing Lily to brunch.

But I looked at Micah. He seemed to feel he had to stick with me. I realized I could give him a way out. "I just used the last of the food they sent. I'm going to stop at the pet store after Dad's. So maybe we should each drive ourselves."

"How about we drive together and I come to the pet store with you?" Micah didn't seem to recognize a way-out when he saw one.

"Micah, you signed on as my attorney, not my bodyguard."

He shrugged. "I'm multitalented."

"Fine. But after we get back from the store, you need to go about your business while I do some work. Sundays and Mondays are the quietest days in the studio." I wanted to spend some time studying my wall. Somewhere in all that there was a clue to who my caller was.

And every woman on my list could be safely X'd out. There was no way that voice was a woman trying to disguise herself as a man.

Something in the way he'd said my name niggled at the corners of my mind. Someone I knew?

"Deal," Micah said, pulling me from my thoughts.

I nodded.

I was showered and dressed by the time Detective Dana arrived.

"You're sure you didn't recognize the voice?" she asked.

"There was something. He was trying to disguise his voice, but for a moment, I thought...well, there was something. I almost thought I had it, but I can't put a finger on it," I said.

"If you come up with anything..." she let her sentence hang there.

"I'll call. I promise." It was an easy promise to make. I just wanted this over with. "And you'll let me know when you get him?"

"Yes." She started toward my front stairs then turned around, "Did anyone else hear your conversation with the mystery man?"

"Adi and Nori were here, but I didn't want to worry them, so I stepped into the kitchen."

She nodded and left.

Micah followed her down and locked the door.

When he came up, I said, "She thinks it's me, doesn't she?"

"She didn't say that," Micah said slowly.

"But if I were the person who stuffed a body in a kiln, then claiming a man called and threatened me would be a good way of trying to throw the police off my scent," I said slowly.

"Maybe," he agreed.

I shook my head. I wondered if I'd just made myself seem guiltier to the detective. There was nothing I could do about it. "Let's head to Dad's and then the store."

Lily rode in a car beautifully.

Dad knelt by her as he opened the door. "And who is this?"

I made introductions and then again to Phyllis.

They both seemed happy to see Micah, that is until my father asked, "So why were you at Harry's this morning?"

"Partly because the cops—"

"A cop," I interjected. "One. Just one. The same one."

"The detective stopped in because Harry got a threatening phone call last night."

I was going to kill Micah.

On the heels of that thought came the realization that people who were murder suspects shouldn't threaten murder out loud. But I thought it. And I gave him the stink eye.

I saw the concern on my father's face. This was what I'd wanted to avoid. I glared at Micah.

"You did?" my father asked. "Why didn't you call me?"

"Because it was just a phone call," I said calmly, trying to reassure him. "And between the security cameras and the dog, I don't think anyone will be breaking into my place anytime soon."

"You still should have called me," my father insisted.

"I was there right after she got the call and spent the night," Micah said, as if that would allay my father's worries. Instead he frowned and Micah added hastily, "On the couch."

"The only other living creature in my bed was Lily," I said, then added, "But Dad, I'm no blushing virgin. I'm an adult. I'm divorced. I don't think you get to question my love life."

At the words love-life my father made a strangled noise and grimaced.

"I don't ask about you and Phyllis. I don't ask what your intentions are, or yours," I added to Phyllis for good measure.

She'd been quiet as a mouse, as if she hoped we'd forget she was there.

"About that," my father said, looking at Phyllis who nodded. "My intention is marriage. Phyllis said yes."

She held out her left hand and a wiggled a lovely blue-stoned engagement ring at me. "I hope you don't mind. We planned to tell you while we ate, in a civilized, pleasant manner."

She shot my father a look that had him looking chagrined.

Wow. Phyllis obviously had my father under her spell.

"I'm thrilled," I said. "Congratulations, both of you."

Brunch was filled with Phyllis talking about her wedding plans. Something small. Just family, a few close friends, and family.

"I have a son. Dylan. That means you'll have a brother," she said merrily.

But my father made the tiniest face, which left me thinking this new brother might not be quite what I hoped.

After brunch, we said goodbye and Phyllis made sure we'd both be at Thanksgiving dinner. "I hope Dylan will come as well," she said.

When we got outside, Micah smiled and said, "Let's head to the pet store."

"No. I think we're heading home. I'll drop you off so you can get your car. Then Lily and I will go shopping."

"But I thought we were going togeth—"

"You tattled on me like we were ten-year-olds." My annoyance had bubbled over through brunch. Now that we were out of earshot, I didn't try to hold it in. "I've felt that you and I were spending too much time together too fast, and I think I was right. I think we need some space. So, thank you for everything you've done for me. I'll call if I need legal representation."

"How about if you don't need legal representation?" he asked.

I didn't know. I honestly didn't know. I liked Micah, a lot. But once upon a time I'd liked Alex, too.

Sometimes liking wasn't enough.

My father had always felt he knew what was best for me. I didn't want that again. I wanted a man who would trust me to know what I wanted and to be competent enough to accomplish it.

Micah didn't seem to feel that was the case.

Granted, I needed someone to wire the new security cameras, but I could have hired someone to do it.

"Harry?" Micah asked, pulling me back from my circular thoughts.

"I don't know, Micah. I just don't know."

I pulled into my parking lot next to his car. "I think we both just need a breather."

"What if you get another call from your heavy breather?" he asked.

"Phone calls can't hurt me. I've got strong locks, security cameras, Detective Dana's phone number, and Lily. I think I figured out how to record a call on my phone, so I'll do that, and the detective will know I'm not faking. To be honest, I hope he does call. No matter what, I'll be fine."

"I'm sorry I *tattled*," he said using my word.

"Me, too." He gave me one more weird look, then got out of the car.

"Call me or text me in a few days? Just to let me know you're all right?"

I wanted to say no, but that seemed churlish, so I nodded.

I waited while he got into his car. Then Lily and I went to the store. I knew I'd done the right thing, but everything in me wanted to text Micah and say, *I'm over it, come back.*

But I didn't.

Lily seemed to sense my conflicting feelings and put her large head on my shoulder as I drove.

Dogs were so much easier than people.

Chapter Thirteen

*"Opening the kiln makes me feel like
I did on Christmas morning as a kid.
One part excitement mixed with
more than a little hope, plus a bit of worry
that whatever gift I wanted wasn't
going to be under the tree."*
~Harry's Pottery: A Personal Journey

Barnabas came over late Sunday afternoon to check over Lily. He walked into what amounted to a dog's version of Christmas morning.

It turned out Lily felt all dog toys with squeakers must be annihilated. Two carcasses were now lovingly placed in her dog bed while the stuffing made my tiny living room floor look as if a snowstorm had swept through it.

I wasn't sure how Lily would behave with strangers, but it was love at first sight with Barnabas.

"Aren't you a beauty?" he murmured as he pet her and checked her out.

"The foundation said she was current on all her shots and gave me the paperwork," I told him and handed them over.

He looked them over, still stroking Lily's head. "I'll start a file for her at work and get her in the system."

I remembered thinking the other day that Barnabas liked Adi and vice versa. I decided to test my theory, I said as nonchalantly as I could, "Adi got a dog for Nori, too."

He looked up with interest. "She did?"

"A much smaller dog than Lily Potter here. Miss Muffet. She has a black spider marking on her back," I added. "I'm sure she'll be bringing the puppy in for a checkup."

"Maybe I should call and see if they'd like me to stop by and check her out? I know Adi's got a crazy schedule and it might make her life a bit easier," he said.

I wondered if he was talking to me or himself?

Either way, I forced myself to contain my grin and said, "I'm sure Adi would appreciate it. Nori's absolutely in love with Miss Muffet."

"I don't have her number," he said, looking at me.

I pulled out my cell and texted him Adi's contact information. "There you go."

"Maybe I'll just text her. That doesn't seem as intrusive as calling." He tapped quickly on his phone. More quickly than I'd have managed.

"Offering to help someone you like isn't intrusive," I said.

"I..." He looked at me as if he were going to deny liking Adi, but then said, "Do you think she noticed?"

I shook my head. "No. Sometimes people are blind to what's right in front of them. So maybe you should tell her how you feel?"

He shrugged. "I know she's been through a lot with her ex. Now that he's out of jail, I know he's still giving her issues. I'm not sure she's ready to date and I don't blame her at all."

I suspected that Adi might like him, too. She always seemed a bit brighter when he walked in the room. "Barnabas, you are nothing like her ex, and that's a huge compliment. He dropped off Nori the other day early, mainly because she was annoying him, I suspect. Listen, why don't you just ask Adi? Ask her out on a date. Nori can come spend the evening with me, so you'll already have a babysitter lined up."

If I were a mother about to start dating again, babysitters would be an issue. And I knew Adi didn't have any discretionary money. She lived paycheck to paycheck with her computer work and the occasional days she worked for me and the sporadic child support Kev gave her.

"Really? You'll babysit?" Barnabas asked.

"Really," I assured him.

He seemed lost in thought for a moment, then a small smile grew into a larger one as he said, "I think I just might."

As if on cue, his phone beeped. He looked down. "She said she'd appreciate it and sent me her address."

Normally when Barnabas came over, he lingered and hung out. We had a big brother—little sister relationship. Or maybe big sister—little brother.

Siblings.

If I had an opportunity to pick a sibling, I'd have picked Barnabas.

I hoped I liked my new *brother* half as much.

But today, Barnabas had no interest in hanging out with his surrogate sister after that text from Adi. He left with a huge grin on his face and me calling, "Good luck" after him.

Afterwards, I took Lily's second dog bed downstairs to my studio and put it in the back corner, away from the bulk of the mess. I wanted to see how she'd behave in the studio.

She followed me down and promptly went on a sniffing spree throughout the shop. And then that was it.

She plopped on her new bed and watched me for a second before she promptly fell asleep.

That was the moment I decided adopting an older dog rocked.

I thought about working on a piece, but instead I went and stood in front of my idea board.

I kept thinking that it wasn't *what* I was missing, it was *who*.

Who else could have access to a key?

Who?

I'd crossed off my *Wine and Mud* ladies, even though I had no proof they hadn't done it.

I'd crossed off my father and Miss Betty.

I'd crossed off Trisha and her in-jail husband.

Who?

Hap?

He's lied to Kitty by not telling her he was out of work. If he'd lie about something like that, what else might he lie about?

I was going to do some checking, but I seriously couldn't see Hap killing anyone.

The voice from the call that I almost recognized.

"Harry," he'd said.

Someone I knew at least casually.

Round and round and round my thoughts tumbled.

So much had happened in the last couple weeks.

A body, an investigation, Micah, my dad dating and getting engaged to Phyllis...

It was obvious that while I had many fine qualities, being an investigator wasn't one of them.

Erie's Quincy Mac had turned her investigative skills into a new career in Hollywood. That was fine for her. But I didn't want a new job. I had the job of my dreams. Adding investigator to my skill set wasn't a priority. I just wanted this over.

I dropped my makeshift cover over my idea board. I was going to trust Detective Dana would figure out who-dunnit.

I was an ex-lawyer, current-potter, and I was taking my life back.

I walked over to my bucket of clay and was thankful I hadn't reached in yet because my phone beeped.

I hoped it was Barnabas asking me to babysit.

It wasn't.

It was a blocked number.

Fearing it was my mystery caller, I resolutely didn't pick up, hoping it would go to voicemail.

The phone stopped ringing and moments later, I got a beep notifying me I had a message.

I picked up. The voice was even more disguised than last time, or else it was someone else entirely.

"If you don't drop it, you might find your new kiln works as well as the old one for disposing of bodies."

It felt as if I'd been sucker punched. As if all the oxygen had been expelled and I had no way to draw in any new air.

I couldn't breathe.

For a moment, I sat there staring at my phone with fear coursing through my body.

But the fear burned out quickly and all that was left was rage.

I didn't ask for any of this.

For two weeks, I'd been asking myself who killed poor Junior and stuffed him in my kiln. My life circled around that question. The one thing I had learned was I was not Quincy Mac.

I called Detective Dana.

I didn't call Micah.

As an attorney, that was dumb. I knew it was dumb.

But as a woman who he'd felt he could tattle on? Yeah, I wasn't calling him.

I reassured myself that it was okay because I wasn't being questioned, I was offering up new evidence in an ongoing case.

I was a witness.

Half an hour later, Detective Dana arrived in a dress that said she hadn't been on duty.

"I'm so sorry. I obviously interrupted something. This could have waited until tomorrow."

She frowned. "I'll tell you what I told my date, my job doesn't wait. It's important. It's as important as anything he does."

She sighed. "Sorry, that came off very defensive. But he seemed to feel that taking me out to dinner a few times meant he had to become the center of my universe. That won't ever work for me."

"Men," I said in sympathy.

"Men," she agreed. Then she turned professional. "About the call?"

I opened my phone and played the voicemail over the speaker.

"I know it could be argued that after our last conversation, I set this up. I could have bought a burner phone and somehow disguised my voice to throw you off track. Only I didn't. I don't know if you have some way of copying the message or tracking the caller. But if you need to borrow my phone, you're welcome to it. No warrant or anything."

She looked at me. "You understand I still have to consider you a suspect."

"Yes. And a certain attorney would be annoyed that I didn't call him, but I'm over his highhanded ways. I am competent and I realize what I'm offering. I didn't do this. There's nothing on my phone that could incriminate me."

I could almost picture Micah's disapproving expression as I said the words.

"And you're willing to sign your phone over to me anyway?" Detective Dana asked.

"Yes. The attorney in me knows it's not the smartest move, but the potter who just wants her life back doesn't care. I didn't do it. There's nothing on that phone to show I did it. There is however something on that phone from the person who presumably did do it or knows the person who did do it, so you can have it."

She eyed me as if trying to decide if I was crazy, innocent, a horrible lawyer, or what.

"But I would like it back asap though." I added. "My life is on that phone."

She smiled and I figured whatever she'd decided, it wasn't that I was the corpse kilner.

Corpse Kilner.

I'm glad I hadn't said that out loud...it was not a funny pun.

"I hear you," she finally said. "I'll take it in now and have our tech guy copy that message first thing tomorrow."

"And if I get another call from a blocked number, feel free to answer it. I know, I could still be the one making the calls to throw you off. Maybe you can think of something to say that will get more information out of him."

"Or her," she said.

"Or me," I added with a grin.

Yeah, I felt pretty sure that Detective Dana might think I was nuts and a sucky lawyer, but she didn't think I was the murderer.

She didn't smile, but I did see a nice glint in her eye. "I'll be in touch tomorrow, first thing."

"Thanks," I said. "And Detective?"

She turned.

"When my ex-husband left me, he said he deserved to be happy and I wasn't making him happy. Truth is, no one can make someone else happy. You have to do that for yourself. But someone who doesn't understand you and doesn't value the work you do...they *can* make you unhappy. You deserve more than a man who doesn't understand what you do is important."

She gave me that look again. I was pretty sure she was leaning towards I was crazy, but there it was. Sometimes everyone needs to hear the truth. And the truth was, what she did for a living mattered.

"Thanks," she finally said. "See you in the morning."

I thought about my lecture to Micah this morning and felt a bit bad about it. He'd be worried if he tried to call my number and got the detective instead of me. And as my attorney, he needed to know what I'd done.

I called him from the shop's line.

"Hello?" he said.

"Micah, it's Harry. I just wanted you to know I got another call—"

"I'll be right over," he said before I even finished the sentence.

"No, you won't," I said quickly. I could almost picture him running to the door as the words came out of his mouth. "I don't need you. I'm fine. I didn't pick up and let the call go to voicemail. Then I immediately called the detective. She left with my phone so she can take the message off. I gave her permission to go through it and use anything that might help."

As expected, he said, "Harry, that's not advisable—"

"Yeah, I know. You keep forgetting that I'm an attorney, too. But this wasn't me acting as an attorney. It's me, who was violated by all this. It was me, whose studio was used for illegal purposes. It's me, who's been threatened. That person—that citizen—turned her phone over to the detective in hopes of helping the investigation. I didn't call for your permission or for your applause. I simply called to inform you. Detective Dana promised to bring my phone back tomorrow."

"It's never smart to give the cops carte blanche to your phone, Harry. It's not a good idea to give them carte blanche to anything."

"That's what an attorney is trained to say. We're trained that there's an adversarial relationship between attorneys and law enforcement. I don't think it has to be that way. Maybe that's why I never had much interest in being a trial lawyer. I want to think both jobs are about justice. They're about what's right and wrong."

"That's naïve," he said.

"Maybe. But turning my phone over is totally reasonable since I have nothing to hide and I'm too old to play games. I just want my life back."

He sighed. "Are you sure that you don't want me to come over?"

"Why on earth would I want that?" I asked snarkily. I was still a bit out of sorts from him tattling to my father which is probably why I added, "I should probably go now. I informed you like any responsible client would inform their attorney. And I'm sure you probably have to call my father real quick and report back to him."

"You're not being fair," he said softly.

"I don't have to be fair. You work for me. Remember that."

He sighed again. He kind of sounded like a balloon with air hissing out. "Call me if you need me. I don't like the thought of you in that building with no phone."

"I have a phone. A landline. I'm on it now," I said.

"Still. Call me. I'm here for you. Whenever you want me, you just have to say the word. Just say the word," he repeated.

"I won't be saying *the word*. I won't need you," I assured him as I hung up.

Or maybe I was assuring myself.

Maybe that's what my anger was about. Not so much that Micah tattled to my father, but that I was starting to rely on him.

I'd relied on a man before...and that hadn't made Alex happy.

It hadn't made me happy either.
Lesson learned.

Chapter Fourteen

*"Any potter will tell you that you
can't plan for everything.
You can use the same glaze on the
same clay-body and fire it in the same kiln
in the same way and get something
totally different.
There's a quote about the best laid
plans...
I think Robert Burns must have
been a potter."*
~Harry's Pottery: A Personal Journey

It was a long night. I was beyond thankful for Lily.

It felt as if every time I closed my eyes, I had another nightmare. It seemed to center around the voice of my mystery caller. I still felt as if I should be able to put a name to him.

And I was pretty sure it was a *him*, not just a *her* deepening her voice to disguise her identity and gender.

I gave up on sleep at five a.m., drank half a pot of coffee, without eating anything, which was always a mistake. My stomach felt sour, which didn't help my sleep deprived mood.

Luckily, Lily didn't seem to mind. She went outside, came in and ate her breakfast, then stood at the back stairs, already getting used to my routine.

We went downstairs, I put on my apron, wedged a piece of clay, and sat at the wheel.

I'd made my first cup when someone rang the doorbell.

The shop was closed on Mondays, but even if it had been opened, it was only six thirty, so the odds of it being a customer was slim to nil. But Detective Dana had said she'd drop off my phone, so I wiped my hand on a towel and went to the door. No one was on the porch, but I could make out a shadowy figure walking down the block.

Shadowy figure sounded as ominous as seeing that tall man hustling away from my house felt. If I'd had my phone, I would have grabbed a screen shot from the camera.

I hated to admit it, but Micah was right, I should have held onto it.

Feeling shaken, I went back to my wheel and made a dozen mugs. I was just about to start pulling handles for them, when my doorbell rang again.

I went back through the shop and peered out the window. It was the detective.

"I'm so glad you're here. I hope you brought my phone." If shadow man came back, I could grab a picture of him.

"I did," she said as she held it out. "I had our tech guy grab what he needed first thing. Why are you so rattled?"

She was perceptive, which was probably why she was a detective.

"It's probably nothing. I'm edgy. I tossed and turned all night. But someone was at my door at six thirty, ringing the bell. They left and were walking down the block before I answered. It sounds stupid saying it out loud, but it felt ominous at the time. I didn't open the door to call after them."

"What could you make out?" she asked.

"Not much. It was still dark. Just that it was a man and my impression was he was tall, but I have nothing to base that on. His back was facing me, so I don't have any more description than that."

"Okay. If he comes back, call me," she said.

"Wait. Micah and Barnabas put in that new security system. There's a camera," I assured her. I went to the app and checked the footage. Disappointed, I showed it to her. Neither of us could make out his face.

"Send me the file anyway?" She made the order sound like a question.

"Sure."

"And call me if he comes back."

"I will," I promised.

I wondered if I should call Micah and hash this out with him?

At that point, Lily got up and came over to sniff the detective's hand. She knelt down and pet the big dog. "She really is sweet."

"She is," I said. "I think the only reason I got any sleep last night was because she was here.

She got up and said, "I feel better knowing she's here with you."

"To be honest, so do I."

Detective Dana left and I felt better with my phone in my pocket.

The rest of the morning was quiet. No one called. No one came back to my door.

And that should make me happy, but I missed having Micah check in. I knew I should call him, but I hesitated.

If I couldn't figure me out, I couldn't expect him to.

I was mulling that over as I made a sandwich for lunch. My stomach was still experiencing the aftereffects of too much coffee and too little food. I hoped the bread would sop up the acid.

I'd just finished when my cell rang. It was Adi.

"Hey, you. What's up?" I said more cheerily than I felt.

"Listen, I told you that I was going away for just Thanksgiving, but I think I'll be staying a bit longer than I intended. I know that the weekend after is the craziest couple days of the year and I hate to leave you in a lurch, but I just need to get away for a time."

Adi had been heading to Philadelphia to spend the holiday with her folks, but she always said though she loved them, they got along much better when there was an entire state between them. You couldn't go any farther away from Erie than Philadelphia and still be in the state.

"What happened?" I asked.

"Kev came by. I've never seen him like this. He said he knew I'd talked to the cops and wanted to know what I'd said. What could I say to them? I told them that I had a key to your place, but I didn't break in. I didn't put a body in your kiln. And I certainly didn't murder that stranger."

I had a sick feeling in the pit of my stomach as I asked, "What happened?"

"He freaked out. He said I'd betrayed him. He kept saying, 'You don't know what you've done.' He kept muttering things about even when he tried to do the right thing it turned to crap. Everyone was out to get him."

She paused a moment and I could hear her crying. She said, "Harry, it was awful. I've never seen him like that. He was in the middle of his raging when Nori started to cry. He told her he was sorry and it was okay. He held his arms out to hug her, but she wouldn't have anything to do with him. He just looked at me and said, 'I know you don't believe me, but I'd do anything for her. Anything. Stay at your parents for a while, okay?' He left without waiting for my answer or saying anything else. It took me an hour to get Nori calmed down. I don't know what's going on, but I don't want any part of it and I don't want Nori to be in the middle of whatever it is."

"I don't blame you. Go. Get away. I've got things here under control," I said with more confidence than I felt.

"Harry, you don't think he..." Adi started and then stopped.

"No, of course not. He's been in trouble, sure, but not for anything like that. Kev isn't a murderer. He's Nori's father." Even as I said that last part, I realized that it wasn't exactly true. He was indeed Nori's biological parent, but biology doesn't make a father. Time and love does.

Kev had been around a lot more lately and I felt small admitting to myself that it felt more like he wanted a reason to spend time with Adi than he wanted to parent his daughter.

"Take whatever time you need. I'll make it work here. When you come back, you have a job. You'll always have a job with me."

"Thanks, Harry," she said.

"Give my favorite girl a kiss and take care of yourself," I said.

The shop was closed on Thursday for the holiday, but I'd intended to spend Friday and Saturday with Adi and Nori. I'd bought a turkey breast to make, so we'd have *leftovers*. And I was making pies for Dad's and planned on making extra for us. Nori was a whipped cream addict. Hot chocolate was our beverage of choice in cold weather. And of course, hot chocolate required whipped cream. Whenever I used it, I always squirted a generous dollop straight into her mouth and Adi always scolded both of us, which made us laugh.

I figured I'd still cook that turkey breast, but I'd freeze meal-sized portions for later.

I felt very much alone.

Dad had Phyllis, and though I knew he'd come running if I called, I wouldn't. That wasn't how our relationship worked.

I'd pushed Micah away. He'd said all I had to do was say the word and he'd come running.

Part of me was tempted to text him an apology and say, "*The Word*."

But the other part of me knew I didn't want to ever rely on a man again.

I knew Barnabas would come over and hang if I called, but he was busy with his own life and his own job.

I thought about him and Adi. Maybe...

The thought of them together made me smile.

Then I thought about Kev.

I'd taken a roundabout way to get to him because Kev was someone I didn't want to think about. Because once I started thinking, I knew where those thoughts would take me.

Who?

That has been my question.

Kev was angry at Adi and wanted to know what she'd told the cops...as if he had something to be worried about.

I'd left my idea wall covered, but now I took down the cover and remembered my question. It wasn't *what* I was missing, it was *who?*

What if the *who* I was missing was Kev?

I tried to figure out what his motive could be.

I didn't think he was the kind of guy who just went around murdering people, though I didn't have much to base that on. I tried to think about what Adi had ever told me about him.

She'd kicked him out when she was pregnant with Nori, so I'd never known them as a couple. I'd only known him as Adi's ex.

He'd been in prison for a year. Then last year, he mysteriously got released early. Adi said something about being surprised he was at her door.

Why had he been in jail?

Theft.

And Junior's father was in jail for fencing.

Of course, that didn't really make for much of a motive. Even if Junior's father had been the one to fence the items Kev stole, why would Junior be murdered?

It still wasn't a motive.

I moved Kev's Post-It to the center of my board.

Then I moved Senior's Post-It next to his.

What connection was there between them?

I wrote, *stolen items* on a Post-It and stuck it by Kev.

I wrote *fence* on another and put it by Senior.

That still didn't do anything to connect Junior and any of this.

I realized I didn't know where Kev had worked since he got out of jail.

Could there be a connection?

I must have stood in front of my idea board a bit too long for Lily's liking because she bumped into my leg and I reached down to scratch her head.

She turned and looked hopefully at the door.

I smiled. "You want to go for a walk?"

She did a dainty little dance to indicate that yes she did.

"Come on."

I grabbed a jacket and her lead. I double-checked the lock as I went out.

It felt like it might snow.

I don't know that I could explain what upcoming snow felt like, but it was definitely cold enough for snow.

Winters in Erie could be brutal. It was easy to stay inside and just hibernate, but I had a feeling Lily wasn't going to put up with that this year.

She didn't seem to mind the stiff Canadian wind blowing across the lake at all as she pranced her way down Front Street.

"Harry," a voice called. I turned around and there was Miss Betty waving from her door.

We backtracked. "Hi, Miss Betty. I was going to call you. Thursday is probably out for the grocery store, but what about Wednesday?"

"That's why I flagged you down. My niece called and they're coming to pick me up tomorrow. I'll spend the rest of the week at her house, so you won't need to worry about taking me. You get a week off."

"I enjoy our nights out," I said. She looked skeptical, but it was the truth. "Why don't you call me when you get back from your nieces. Buffalo?" I asked.

She shook her head. "The other direction...Cleveland. I will."

"Happy Thanksgiving, Miss Betty," I said.

"Happy Thanksgiving, Harry. Try not to get in any trouble while I'm gone."

I laughed. "I'll do my best. Lily will make sure I toe the line."

She patted the dog who looked adoringly at my neighbor. "I'm sure she will."

"Have a wonderful time."

"You, too dear."

Lily and I walked down Front Street, to State Street then down along the Bayfront Highway. The bay was wavy and wild. Just the kind of day I liked.

I know some people preferred sunny days, but I'd always loved dark, windy days. I liked grey skies. Which was good because Erie had those kinds of days a lot.

I wondered if I liked those kinds of days so much and thus Erie suited me, or if having lived in Erie all my life, other than a brief stint in law school, I'd learned to love those kinds of days.

I was pretty sure it was a chicken or the egg sort of thing.

And in the end, it didn't matter. I liked overcast skies.

Speaking of overcast, I realized that Kev was casting a shadow on everything.

Could he have something to do with Junior?

Adi had had a key to my place.

Kev occasionally had access to her house because of Nori.

Could he have made a copy of her key to my house and...dragged a dead body into the studio trying to destroy the evidence?

It sounded implausible to me.

Of course, someone did just that.

My phone beeped.

It was a text message from Micah. *Any chance you're interested in saying "The Word" yet?*

The Word.

I smiled as I stared at the screen.

I was tempted to text back, *The Word*, but I...

I was afraid.

I was afraid to need him.

So, in the end I simply texted back, *I need more time to figure myself out.*

I'll wait. Just remember, all you have to do is say the word.

For a few moments, I forgot all about my worries and toyed with the idea of texting him back just those two words.

It would be as easy as that. But I still worried that things with Micah had moved too fast.

I still worried that I'd start depending on someone again.

I worried.

Then I thought about my father and all the lonely years he'd spent between my mother and Phyllis.

I didn't want to get so wrapped up in the past that I forgot to live in the present. Even more than that, look to the future.

"Oh, Lily, what am I going to do?"

She paused a moment at the sound of her name, then resumed her sniff-a-thon.

My new dog was good company, but I suspected she'd never be a great conversationalist.

The snow began coming down heavier and we hurried the rest of our walk.

As I walked up the drive to the back door, I saw there were footsteps on the porch. I looked down and realized those footsteps went down my driveway.

I stopped in my tracks, reached in my pocket and dialed Detective Dana's number. "Harry?" she asked.

"I was out for a walk and there are footprints on my porch and down my drive. I know I'm being ridiculous, but given that someone broke in just a couple weeks ago, I was wondering if you could ask a patrol car to stop by?"

"I'm at the station. I'll be there in a few minutes. Don't go inside without me," she said.

She didn't need to warn me because I had no intention of going into my house on my own. "I won't."

It had only been a couple weeks, but between the security cameras, new locks, and Lily, I had been feeling safe again in my house.

All that was undone by a set of footprints.

The cement was too warm for any discernable details on the trail leading to the back door, but the steps on the porch were visible and they were large with a heavy tread. Work boots?

I'd felt all along that whoever put Junior in my kiln had to be a man.

I felt even more certain now.

A man or a woman with very large feet.

I wear a size nine and always felt my feet were large, but I knew they'd be lost in the giant footprints on my porch.

I realized how dumb it was to be thinking about the size of my feet, but it was easier than thinking about someone possibly lying in wait for me inside my own house.

I was over that.

I thought about calling my father or Micah but decided to wait until the detective did her thing.

She was pulling into my driveway minutes later. "Wait here," she said. "Your keys?"

I handed them over and waited.

She went through the back door and disappeared.

How long should I wait for her to come out before calling for backup for her?

I wished she'd brought a second cop, just so she'd have someone to back her up.

It felt like an hour had passed, but when I checked my watch it had only been five minutes.

The front door to the shop opened and she said, "It's all clear."

I went inside and took off Lily's lead.

"It didn't look like anyone got in from the tracks, but I double-checked to be sure. It looks as if that new security system and those new locks did their job."

"What would someone want with me? I mean, I guess I can understand why someone would want to use my kiln, but me? I don't know anything about it. I've racked my brain for who it could be."

"I saw," she said dryly. She turned and walked into the studio and stood in front of my idea board.

There was nothing left for me to do but follow.

"So why is Kev in the middle of your board now?" she asked.

"I don't like him, which isn't a good enough excuse. I get that," I said before she could. "But Adi had a key to my place and he sometimes was at her house to see his daughter, so he had access. And he's had trouble with the law in the past. He did time. But stealing stuff isn't a good enough reason for murder."

"Which is why Junior's dad is next to Kev?" she asked.

"I was wondering if there was a connection. I wondered about the previous owner of the house. He's been in jail, too. It feels like a lot of people connected to this place have been to jail. I don't want to be one of them."

"I don't think it's you," the detective said kindly.

I sighed. "Thanks. Back to Kev. If he stole stuff, he'd need some way to make money from them. And that's what Junior's father did. Fenced stuff."

She stood there, really studying my board. "That makes sense, but I still don't see how that's a motive for murder."

"Neither do I," I admitted.

"Why are all these people off your list?" she asked, pointing to my students, friends and father.

"I have an answer for that. *Because I'm not a cop.* I don't have to make sense or wait for evidence or alibis. Some of them really don't have the strength to load a body into a kiln. And some...some I just don't believe could do it. I can't think of a motive, but even if I could, I'd have crossed them off because I really just don't believe they did it."

She still stared. "So, this Kev?"

I stared at the board and slowly said, "I don't want it to be him. His daughter Nori is the cutest thing you've ever seen and even if Adi isn't with him, it would hurt her. But really, I can't think of a reason why he'd have killed Junior. I have all these bits, but no way to tie them all together."

"I'll let you in on something...that's what police work is. Finding those bits of information and looking for what ties it all together."

I laughed. "That's how I always worked in school. I collected huge quantities of information and eventually it all coalesced and I found how to make it into a report or whatever I needed. I'd hoped this would work the same way."

Detective Dana turned and looked at me. "It's good work, but Harry, it's *my* work. I don't come into your studio and try to make a pot."

"You could," I offered.

She raised an eyebrow and I added, "I have a *Wine and Mud* class on Fridays. They've become so popular I'm thinking about starting a second one and…" I let the sentence fade because I saw her expression. "That's not what you meant, right?"

"Right," she said.

I nodded. "I get it, but I needed to do something proactive. Whoever broke in here violated my home."

"I understand, but please, trust me to do my job. I'm very good at it," she said.

"Detective—"

"Call me Micci."

"Micci, I just want this over."

"Me, too. So, give me a chance to get to the bottom of things."

I nodded my agreement. "You'll check out Kev?"

"Believe it or not, he was already on my list," she said with a grin. "I really am very good at this."

I sighed. "Fine."

"Concentrate on your shop. Friday must be a big day for you," she said.

"It is. Kev's wife was scheduled to help, but..." Would I be breaching Adi's trust if I told the detective—Micci? I decided Adi wouldn't mind. "She was going out of town to spend the holiday with her family but is extending her visit because of Kev."

"What happened?"

I felt as if I'd said as much as I could. "You can call Adi for more information. I don't want to break confidences, but I also don't want to not give you all the facts about him."

The detective nodded. "Okay, I'll call her and I'll stop back in the morning to check on you. Lock this place down tight."

"That's my plan," I assured her.

"And if anything seems amiss, call me."

"I will," I promised as she left.

I double checked all the doors and windows, then because I was feeling anxious, went to work on some simple bowls. I was hoping that the trees and ornaments I'd made for the season moved, but I was also hoping to sell more than that.

What I made last Christmas season was the biggest chunk of last year's earnings. I was hoping this year would be even better.

I couldn't spend enough time at the wheel.

Bowls and plates were easy because I didn't have to make and attach handles like with mugs. Though mugs sold better.

I'd work on those tomorrow.

Tonight, I wanted mindless work. I wanted the rhythm of production to clear my head.

I wanted this over.

For the next two hours, I made bowls and Lily watched me from her dog bed.

I left all the bowls drying. I'd trim their feet tomorrow.

I took Lily upstairs, fed her and stared at my refrigerator, trying to decide what I should eat.

What I wanted was Micah to cook me something.

I missed him.

I gave up fighting with myself and called him. "Hey."

"Hey," he said. "What's the word?"

I knew he was hoping I'd say *The Word*, but I didn't. I did say, "I'm making dinner and thinking about you."

"I think I'll take that as a compliment. If you think about me every time you eat, that's at least three thoughts a day," he said.

I smiled and admitted, "I might think of you a bit more often than that."

"This conversation is getting better and better. If you like, I could bring you some dinner."

"I would like to see you and the dinner would be a bonus. But—"

"You could have stopped before that *but*. I really don't care for that word at all," he said.

I sighed. "I need to be clear—I'm still concerned about how fast things developed between us. After all, the first time I really met you, I came home with you. I want to slow things down."

"For clarity's sake, I feel I need to point out you slept in my guestroom."

I smiled. "Yes. But even then, there's a chance I didn't want to sleep in the guestroom."

"Better and better," he said softly.

"Still, I don't want to rush things."

"Fine. We'll take things as slow as you like. How about you call me in the evenings and I'll see you at dinner on Thursday at your father's. After that, we'll talk about going out within a reasonable amount of time. Not too soon, not too long."

"I think that sounds like a good idea," I admitted, trying not to tell him just how much I would like it. "Things are going to be crazy here over the weekend. The Black Friday phenomenon is a thing."

I could almost hear him smiling. "If you need help, I can run a register. Well, I can if you show me how yours works. I know they're all a little different."

I laughed. "I'll talk to you tomorrow and we'll see."

"Remember," he said. "I'm here any time. All you have to do is…"

"Say *the word*. I know." I was smiling as well. "Good night, Micah."

"Good night, Harriet."

This time I didn't correct him. I'd been Harry most of my life. Even my mother had called me Harry. My father was the only one who called me Harriet. And now Micah. The way he said my name made it seem as if it was an entirely different one than my father used.

I made some eggs and tried to settle down to read a new book on folk art. It was good, but I couldn't make my mind settle enough to enjoy it.

I turned on the television.

I watched a HeartMark romcom and felt better.

"Come on, Lily. Bedtime," I said. I started down the backstairs to let her out. We were building a rhythm because she followed me with no coaxing.

I opened the door to let her out and as usual, she bound out and then turned and growled.

I looked to see what she was growling at, but at that moment, a hand grabbed me and forced me back inside, slamming the door as Lily charged it.

I heard her hit it.

Then he turned and shut the inside door as well and locked it.

I looked up and saw Adi's ex.

Chapter Fifteen

"Pottery is about the technical side of how to make a piece, but it's more than that. It's the glazing. It's the finish. Without the right ending, the piece falls flat."
~Harry's Pottery: A Personal Journey

"Kev," I said.

I made a break for the door, but he easily blocked me. "I told you to stay out of this."

"I—"

"Be quiet, I have to think. I saw that cop here again."

My heart was racing and my mind was muddled. It felt very much like that morning I found Junior in the kiln. *Think*, I told myself.

"Yes, the cop was here. I'm a suspect," I lied. Micci had pretty much admitted I wasn't a suspect. "She's been coming after me, trying to get me to confess to something I didn't do."

"You're a lawyer. You know better than talking to the cops. I'm not a lawyer and even I know better."

"I haven't been talking to her but that doesn't stop her from pestering me."

"I don't know what to do with you," he said more to himself than to me.

I couldn't decide if that was a good thing or not. He'd already murdered one person.

"You can just walk away. I won't say anything to anyone. I won't tell them you killed Junior."

His head snapped as if I'd hit him. For a moment, I thought he was going to admit or deny it, but instead he said, "I tried to warn you. You put my kid in danger."

"I don't know what you mean." I'd read somewhere that if you were kidnapped you should try to make a connection with the kidnapper. Humanize yourself.

I wasn't sure if this was a kidnapping or he was planning to make the next body in the kiln. Either way, I thought delaying was a good idea. I added, "I would never do anything to put Nori in danger."

"But you did. I tried to warn you off, but you wouldn't listen." He moved toward me and I backed up, trying to stay out of his reach.

"What are you going to do with me, Kev?" I asked, though I wasn't sure I wanted to hear his answer.

"I told you to stop. I told you." He moved towards me again. I countered his movement, putting one of my work tables between us.

"Just leave," I said.

"I can't. I have to protect Nori."

"I love that little girl. She loves me. I'm her Aunt Harry. And I would never do anything to endanger her. You don't have to hurt me. Tell me what I need to do to protect her."

He sighed like a punctured balloon.

"I know," he said. "I told Adi to take Nori out of town for as long as possible."

"I talked to her and that's what she plans to do," I told him.

He sighed again then softly said, "Good. That's a relief."

"Kev, you and I will never be friends, but like I said, I love Nori. Before I was a potter, I was an attorney. Hand me a dollar."

"Why?"

"For a retainer."

He slid the dollar across the table. I watched him, ready to run if he tried to come at me again but he didn't.

"Now what?" he asked.

"Now you tell me what's going on. What kind of mess are you in? Then I'll do what I can to find you another attorney and get you out of it."

"I don't think there's any getting out of it." He looked like he might cry. "I effed it all up."

That's what he said. *Effed.*

I remembered a long while back Adi saying she laid down the law about using profane language in front of the baby.

Obviously, it stuck.

That *eff* moment was the one when some of my fear dissipated.

Micah would say I was being reckless. I suspected my father and Detective Dana—Micci—would agree. Still, I said, "Come upstairs, I'll put on some tea and you can tell me everything. From the beginning."

I hoped that giving him a second would help him get himself under control.

"Do you mind if I let the dog in?" I asked. "The neighbor might think it's suspicious that I left her out in this cold."

That was true but I was also hopeful that if Kev came back after me, Lily would at least get in his way a little.

"Is she going to tear my throat out?" he asked.

"I can't imagine she would."

"Sure," he said.

I let Lily in and she made a low rumbling growl as she looked at Kev but didn't make a move toward him. She stood, glued to my side as I walked up the stairs. I didn't turn around to see if Kev was following but I heard sniffing.

As I put on the teakettle, he sat at the table and Lily finally left me side to go over and put her head on his lap, as if she sensed his emotional distress and wanted to help.

I grabbed a notepad and a pen, then sat down opposite him.

"Okay, the beginning," I said.

"I was young and dumb and thought that stealing stuff was easier than working. I had a job at a used car lot. Yeah, I thought it would be easy, but it wasn't. On weeks when my commission was less than I needed, I filled in the gap by breaking into someone's house or car and supplementing it. That's how I thought about it, supplementing my income. I heard about Steve from some of the guys I worked with. We took cars to his garage and he was good about fixing them well-enough."

"Well enough?" I asked.

"Well enough to hold together long enough to sell them. After that, we didn't care."

I tried very hard to keep any judgments to myself. But he was the kind of man who gave used car salesmen a bad name.

"When the cops caught me, I was looking at least five years. My lawyer said make a deal. And I did."

"That's how Junior's father got caught?" I asked.

"They were already building a case against him. I was just the final nail in the coffin. *His* coffin. I did a year in prison. I've been really working to do better. Then I heard from an old friend that Summers carried a grudge."

There it was. That was the connection.

"My buddy got me a gun and told me to get out of town. All I could think of was Nori. I was going to take his advice and leave town, even if it meant ditching my parole, but I wanted to see Nori one last time. I planned on going over the next morning, then leaving. But that night, Junior showed up. Only I didn't know he was Steve's son. He said, 'This is from my father,' and that's when I knew it was Summer's kid. Then he shot me. He was a bad shot and got me in the leg. I was a better shot when I shot him. It was self-defense, but who's going to buy that?"

The words had spilled out, just a torrent of descriptions as Kev tried to justify what happened. It could be a story, but I believed it.

"I'm buying it." I looked at my notes. "So why my kiln?"

"Adi's talked about your store and studio. She loves it here. And I knew that your kiln got really hot. I looked it up online and kilns go to eighteen or twenty-four hundred degrees. I looked up how hot it has to be to cremate someone. It said fourteen to eighteen hundred. Steve should have been burned up to just a few bone chips. I figured no one could identify him and there'd be no trace evidence left that could lead to me."

"How did you get in?" I asked.

"Adi's key. I stopped to see Nori that next morning and swiped it, then stopped back later that night. Adi was going crazy looking for her keys. I "found" them behind the couch for her."

"You told Adi to leave town?"

"Steve Senior figured out it was me who killed his kid. He's sending someone else after me and I didn't want Adi or Nori caught in the crossfire."

Yes, I believed Kev.

"Did a doctor treat your wound?"

He shook his head. "I pulled the bullet out myself, then super-glued the wound shut."

Wow. I didn't think I'd have been able to do that.

"So now what?" he said, defeat in his voice. "You're going to call the cops?"

"No. I'm going to call another attorney who deals with criminal cases and then we're going to call the cops together. You're going to turn yourself in."

"I had a gun," he said. "That's a violation right there."

"Yes. I can't promise you won't do any more time, but I can promise I'll do my best for you for Nori's sake."

"Thank you," was all he said.

I called Micah's number.

I could hear him smiling as he answered, "Did you call to say *the word*?"

Part of me really did want to say those two words, but first things first. "No. I called about business."

"Business?" Micah asked.

"How would you feel about being co-counsel?"

"With and for...?" he asked.

"With me, and for the person who put Junior in my kiln," I said.

"Seriously, why would you—"

I cut him off. I didn't want to do this one the phone. "Just come over if you're interested."

"I'll be there in ten."

I was going to respond, but he'd already hung up.

Micah got to my door in eight minutes.

"You drove too fast," I scolded.

"Yeah, a speeding ticket is my biggest concern right now." He pulled me into his arms and hugged me. "You scared years of my life. Literally, years."

"I'm sorry. I didn't mean for any of it to happen," I said.

"Why do I feel as if this could become a habit with you?"

"Maybe because I'm about to take you upstairs and introduce you to the Kiln-Killer."

"You have him upstairs? Are you crazy? Did you call Dana?" he barked.

"Yes. No. And no. And before we go any further, let's get something straightened out, I don't take orders from you. I don't need a keeper. Right now, I need someone to help me, and maybe later...we'll talk about that after."

"It wasn't an order," he said through gritted teeth.

"It was close enough," I said. "Hear him out. I'm representing him, but since we've established that I'm better with a contract than this kind of thing, I'm hoping you'll work with me."

"You are crazy."

As I looked at his concerned expression and knew he was scared for me because he cared about me, I admitted to myself I was indeed crazy. Crazy about him.

It was new.

It was fragile.

It might not lead anywhere.

But when I looked at Micah I realized that I hoped it did.

I didn't say any of this.

Instead, I took him back upstairs and asked Kev to run through the entire story again. And Micah listened.

I watched him as he did so and realized he believed Kev, too.

Two hours later, I let Lily outside before I left with Micah and Kev to meet Detective Dana.

We told her that Kev wanted to confess, but we hoped she'd call the DA or an ADA because we wanted to make a deal.

I let Micah do the talking and negotiating because this was his forte.

And when he was satisfied, Kev ran through things a third time.

I listened closely. When someone was lying and providing a story they've made up, there are elements of sameness. They're talking from a script that they've written for themselves. But when it's the truth, there are variations. Information is added or forgotten. Their story has a core of truth without sounding like a script.

Kev had that basic kernel of truth to his story.

There was a lot of talking that Kev and I weren't necessary for.

"Will you tell Adi that I did this for Nori. I know I'll be doing some time, but I'd do anything to keep her from being hurt."

"I will." I thought about Barnabas and asked, "Do you still have feelings for Adi?"

It was cheeky and none of my business, but I was Adi and Barnabas' friend, so maybe it was.

He shook his head. "No."

Kev didn't need me to say anything. He shot me a little smile. "I just hope I'm a cautionary tale for her."

And for one brief moment, I saw what Adi must have seen once upon a time when she looked at Kev.

"When this is over, you can make a new start," I said.

"It sounds like it will be a long time before it's over, but I tried to make it right for Nori. Remind her of that as she gets older."

"I will," I promised.

"And you'll look out for them?" he asked.

"Absolutely."

"I'm sorry for what I put you through."

It had been horrific, but as I looked at Micah, I realized that something good had come out of it. "I'll be fine."

They took Kev away to process him. "I'll be tied up with Kev for a while," Micah said, "but when I'm done, I was wondering if you'd—"

I cut him off with two simple words. "*The Word.*"

He understood. And he kissed me. I mean, really kissed me. This wasn't some sweet introduction. It was a true, knee-buckling kiss that spoke of wanting more on both our parts.

It was fireworks on the Fourth of July sort of kiss.

It was everything a kiss should be.

I grinned as we broke apart.

He was grinning as well. "I'll call you as soon as I can."

I wanted to savor and relive that kiss, but I knew I had a call to make of my own. I needed to put everything to rights before I started thinking about what to do about Micah.

I went home, curled up next to Lily and made myself get it over with.

Calling Adi was one of the most difficult phone calls of my life.

I didn't try to sugarcoat anything. She deserved the truth. The whole truth.

I wasn't sure what I expected, but she was silent as I laid out Kev's story. "I hope the fact that he came forward on his own carries some weight, but he'll have to serve the rest of his original sentence and even if they buy his self-defense story, which I do, there will be charges about the gun. Micah's his attorney. He'll give him the best representation. And he has the DA's promise Kev will serve his sentence at a different facility than Steve Summers."

"I'm so sorry you went through all that. It's my fault," Adi said.

"Adi, it's not." It was Kev's fault, but to be honest, I was hard pressed to feel bitter about that.

I started to say it's-okay and then I realized it wasn't for Kev. It wouldn't be okay for him for a long time.

"Can I do anything?" I asked.

"I know I could come home like I planned, but if you don't mind, I'd like to spend some time here with my family," she said.

"Of course, I don't mind. Take all the time you need. I meant what I said earlier, you have a job waiting for you when you come back."

"Thanks, Harry. Happy Thanksgiving."

I didn't return the phrase because I didn't think Adi's Thanksgiving would be very happy at all. I simply said, "Call me if you need me."

"I will," she promised.

I added, "And call me even if you don't."

"I will. Bye, Harry."

Adi said the words in a way that made me wonder if she was ever coming back. I would miss her, but I suspected Barnabas would miss her even more.

I hung up and sat on the couch, not sure what to do next.

The mystery was solved.

I didn't actually solve it, but I'd come to realization that Kev was my primary suspect, so I sort of did.

The good news was no one was out to get me now.

"Come on, Lily," I said. I went downstairs and pulled out a hunk of clay. I didn't have anything in mind, I simply wedged it and studied it for a long moment, then had an idea.

When I had the basic shape done, I put it in front of the fan. I turned it every ten minutes or so, and soon, I had a leather-hard piece. That meant I could carve it at will.

And I did.

About an hour later, my phone buzzed, indicating someone was at my apartment's door. I glanced at the screen and saw it was Micah.

I grabbed my project and went to the studio door. I opened it and called across the porch, "Over here."

"You've been working," he said.

I realized I must look like a mess, but to be honest, I didn't care. I nodded and as he stepped inside, I held my project out for him.

I'd hand-formed a giant coffee mug, which was much less precise than throwing one. But it summed up how I was feeling—less precise. I wasn't quite sure about anything, but I knew what I wanted.

I'd carved *The Word* over and over on the mug. Big letters. Small letters. Bold letters. Soft and hesitant letters.

It pretty summed up my feelings.

"It will still need to be bisque fired, then glazed, then—"

Micah apparently didn't care what else it needed. He interrupted me and said, "It's perfect. And so are you."

I didn't disabuse him of the notion, though I knew I was a lot less than perfect.

I couldn't have disabused him if I wanted to because he was kissing me.

Which was just fine, because I was kissing him back.

Chapter Sixteen

"When I start a project, I have an image in my mind. I know how I hope it turns out. But my most amazing projects are ones that end up being something entirely different than what I'd envisioned."
~Harry's Pottery: A Personal Journey

"We're getting married," my father said.

I dropped my turkey-skewering fork and looked at Phyllis's son, my new soon-to-be brother. He did not look impressed, though dad and Phyllis both glowed with happiness.

I couldn't remember ever seeing my father look happier. "Yes, I know," I said. "I'm thrilled."

"I know I told you we were engaged, but now I'm telling you we're getting married soon."

"How soon?" I asked.

"Before Christmas," Phyllis said. "Judge Stephanie said she'd officiate and..."

I felt the glow of happiness as I listened to her plans. I looked across the table. Dylan was not glowing in the least...he was glowering.

He didn't raise a glass or say anything. He just bowed his head and continued to plow through the food his mother had prepared.

Phyllis's son had no manners.

My soon-to-be brother.

I'd always wanted a sibling, but Dylan wasn't what I had in mind.

I cheered myself up with another bite of turkey.

"So, Harry, you're sure this is over?" my father asked as he served my pumpkin pies.

"Kev's back in jail, so yes, I think so. Tomorrow things are going to be nuts at the shop...well, I hope they're nuts. It was last year. Adi's staying in Philly a bit longer, so it's going to be even crazier than I thought it would be."

"The joys of being a small business owner," my father said.

"Harry, if you need a hand, I'd be happy to come over for a while," Phyllis offered. "The office is closed until Monday, so I have the time. It would be fun."

"Seriously?" I asked.

"Seriously," she said with a gentle smile. "You'd be doing me a favor and we'd have some time to get to know each other."

That sounded perfect to me.

"Then yes. Yes, I accept," I said.

The four-way conversation began again in earnest as we all ate a tremendous amount of food. My father was going to put on some serious weight if he let Phyllis do all the cooking.

It was only a four-way conversation because Dylan didn't say anything. He just continued staring at his plate and eating.

I wasn't going to let a dour new brother-to-be keep me from my glee. I ate, I talked and enjoyed the day, partly because I could tell my father was so happy, partly because I was just that happy sitting by Micah.

I realized I had a lot to be thankful for.

"I wondered if it would be weird or if you'd mind if I took a class?" Phyllis asked. "Your father spoke of what you do with such pride—I couldn't help but want to try it myself."

She dropped her voice to a stage-whisper and said, "He won't drink out of any other mug than one you've made."

I would have placed a bet that the darkening in my father's cheeks was a blush.

"I would love to have you in class. My Friday night *Wine and Mud* class is full, but I've had a bunch of new people sign on for classes." Both Trisha and Detective Dana—Micci—had signed up. "I was thinking about starting a weeknight class."

"Let my name be the first one on that new class list," Phyllis said.

Yes, I had a lot to be thankful for this year.

When I'd read about how Erie's own Quincy Mac had found her writing passion because of the first murder she cleaned, I'd thought that my *View to a Kiln* wouldn't lead me to any new passion because I'd already found my passion with pottery.

I was right about that, but I was wrong about it too because the body in my kiln led me to Micah. And I was pretty passionate about him.

When dinner was over, Dylan went out to the living room to watch football while my father went into the kitchen to help Phyllis. Micah and I were clearing the table and he whispered, "*The word.*"

I gladly stepped into his arms.

As he kissed me, I was pretty sure, he was passionate too.

So, I'd followed in Quincy's shoes that way.

But I was hoping that's where the similarity ended because I had no interest in ever finding another dead body or solving a murder again.

No interest at all.

Dear Reader, Thank you so much for picking up A View to a Kiln! I hope you enjoyed the first book in my new cozy mystery series. I mentioned Quincy Mac in the story. If you've never read about her adventures, you can check them out.

Maid In LA:

1. Steamed

2. Dusted

3. Spruced Up

4. Swept Up

5. Polished Off

ABOUT THE AUTHOR

Award-winning author Holly Jacobs has
over three million books in print worldwide.
The first novel in her Everything But. . . series,
Everything But a Groom, was named one of
2008's Best Romances by Booklist, and her
books have been honored with many other
accolades. She lives in Erie, Pennsylvania,
with her family. You can visit her at
www.HollyJacobs.com.

Made in the USA
Middletown, DE
09 February 2022